Phantom Horse
Goes to Ireland

Phantom Horse
Goes to Ireland

Christine Pullein-Thompson

RAVETTE BOOKS

Phototypeset by Input Typesetting Ltd, London
Printed and bound in Great Britain
for Ravette Books Limited,
3 Glenside Estate, Star Road,
Partridge Green, Horsham,
West Sussex RH13 8RA
by Cox & Wyman Ltd,
Reading

ISBN 1 85304 117 3

1

We had just returned from school. Angus had thrown his briefcase down in the hall. Outside, the garden was full of flowers, the lawn peppered white with daisies, yellow roses bedecking the side of the cottage. The ponies were standing nose to tail in the paddock. It was one of those days when it seemed impossible that summer would ever end.

"Dad wants to talk to you in the sitting-room," Mum called. "He's come back early. There's going to be another upheaval."

"Oh no!" I shrieked. "We are not going to have to move again?"

"I'm still doing my exams, Angus said.

"And Moonlight is going to foal next week," I added. "And what about Phantom?"

"They will survive," replied Mum.

"But we've only been back from America a year," I answered.

"Come in and stop arguing," called Dad from the sitting-room.

He was pacing the carpet, his hands plunged deep in his trouser pockets. He had changed out of his London clothes. He looked on edge, like a horse lining up for a race.

"We've made plans for the summer," said Angus. "Moonlight's expecting."

"I've got to go to Nigeria," replied Dad. "I know it's a bore. But there's been a kidnapping. I've been asked to take over."

"You mean the one in the paper?" asked Angus, suddenly serious, "The one everybody's talking about?"

I stared at Dad. For a moment I couldn't speak. Then I said, "Supposing you're kidnapped?"

"I shan't be. I shall have special protection. But they won't be responsible for you too, so you can't come. That's the problem."

"It doesn't matter. We will be all right here with Mum," I replied quickly. "Though we'll be worried about you of course. We'll help with the washing-up and dig the garden, and we won't do anything silly while you're away. I promise."

Mum was staring at the carpet as though all the answers to everything were there. Without looking at her face I knew that she was upset. "I won't even ride in the Horse Trials if you like," I continued with a choke in my voice, knowing how Mum hated me jumping fixed fences. "I'll ride Phantom quietly and sensibly. We'll both be sensible, won't we, Angus?"

My brother, with his dark brown hair and brown eyes, was looking thoughtful. "I wouldn't mind going to Nigeria. I think you're jolly lucky, Dad," he said.

"Mum's coming too; not at once, but soon. I'm leaving tonight," said Dad, turning to face us for the first time. "I'm flying from Heathrow."

I looked at Angus. "We'll be OK on our own. I'm of a responsible age now," he said. "Nothing awful can happen to us here."

"Your Aunt Nina has promised to come for a few days," Mum told us, "and then you're going to Ireland. My cousin is going to have you to stay. She's very nice. She lives in the wilds and has a girl about your age. She wrote at Christmas saying, 'Visit at any time. We never

6

see you', so we've taken her up on it. We phoned her an hour ago. It's all fixed up."

"What about the ponies?" I asked. "I can't leave Phantom."

"He's going, too," replied Dad. "My secretary is arranging everything. You'll leave in a week or two, before the end of term. Gosh, look at the time. I had better finish packing. I envy you; it will be so peaceful and the fishing is marvellous. Besides you can talk horse till the cows come home."

My mind was in a whirl. All my plans for the summer had been swept away as easily as chalk off a blackboard. I imagined rolling hills, banks, a peaceful river.

"Dad's cousin married someone we didn't like," Mum said. "Now she and her daughter are on their own and rather lonely. I expect she will be glad of company."

I saw myself leaping across banks on Phantom. We might even get some cub-hunting, and somewhere in Ireland there must be a horse for Angus. I started to feel better. I looked at Mum and saw that she was smiling.

"Please don't be kidnapped," I said. "It would be too awful for words."

"I shall be all right," Mum answered. "They've got their man already. They've made their point."

I changed out of my school dress into jeans and a shirt and went out to the paddock. The sky was still blue except for a few small fluffy clouds floating like whipped egg in the sky. Birds were singing quietly as they do in the evening. Somewhere a cow was lowing. I put my arms round Phantom's neck and told him about Ireland. He licked my pockets and nuzzled my hair. "We will be back here in time for the apples," I told him. "I expect you'll have to fly again. Please behave yourself this time."

7

Last year we had brought him home from Virginia, USA. We had flown from Kennedy Airport and he had had to be drugged for the journey. For an awful moment it had seemed that we were all going down into the Atlantic. It was a moment I would never forget, a memory which would haunt me all my life.

Moonlight would be foaling soon. I hoped that she would have a grey like herself. It would be Angus's foal. My old pony, Mermaid, had promised to be the nanny, or so Angus said. He looked at Moonlight night and morning. "You must hurry," I told her now, "because soon you will have to go to the farm. We will be gone." She looked very peaceful, as though she had everything she wanted in life, whereas Phantom was as restless as ever, nudging me, gazing into the distance, looking for new fields to conquer.

Mum was calling me from the house now. "Are you coming to Heathrow?" she called. "Because you had better change."

"All right," I shouted back. "But must I change? Won't jeans do?"

Heathrow was full of people. Dad's secretary was already there with a briefcase full of papers for him.

She said, "Will you excuse me for a few minutes, Mrs Simpson? I must just explain a few things to your husband."

We stood looking at the bookstalls and I had a lump in my throat which wouldn't go. "I hate airports," Mum said. "They give me the shivers."

Dad and his secretary, Melinda, rejoined us. "Your plane leaves from gate number eight," she said presently. "Here are the tickets and landing-card. I will just check in your baggage."

"Now don't worry," Dad told us. "I'm well briefed.

I shall have a detective with me on and off. I shall be perfectly safe."

"Touch wood," exclaimed Angus.

They were calling passengers to his plane now. We watched him go through gate number eight and Mum said, "That's it. '*Home John, and don't spare the horses*'."

"I wish we could see him take off," Angus said.

We found our car in the car-park and Mum drove home. The sun was setting above the Chilterns and everything looked indescribably beautiful—the hedges white with hawthorn blossom, the chestnuts white and pink, and the fields deep in lush green grass. Nigeria will be very barren after this, I thought; poor Dad!

Angus went straight to the orchard to look at Moonlight; presently I heard him calling, "She's foaled. It's trotting about. She's done it all by herself. She's foaled . . ."

"It's very early," called Mum rushing outside. "We should have put her by herself."

"It's all right. It's a filly," shouted Angus.

I ran to the orchard. The foal looked tiny, and was still wet and a little unsteady on her legs. She had a long delicate head and small ears. Mermaid was keeping Phantom away. He stood alone under an apple tree, not daring to approach nearer.

"That's another bridge crossed," said Mum in a satisfied voice.

"I shall call her Twilight," Angus told us, "because she was born in the evening, which is most unusual according to all the books I've read on the subject."

I looked at the tall elms. There was a pigeon in one saying over and over again, "My toe bleeds Betty . . ." It was a peaceful sound; everything was peaceful. "I wish we could stay here forever," I said.

"I wish Dad wasn't in the Foreign Office. I don't want to leave Twilight," Angus answered.

"You've got a little longer," Mum said. "And be polite to Aunt Nina. You know she hates it here. The country bores her stiff, so make allowances."

I thought of Aunt Nina; she wore strange hats and false eyelashes and talked endlessly about Embassy parties. She was Dad's sister and worked in the Civil Service.

"She'll hate us," Angus answered. "I don't see why she has to be here. We're old enough to be on our own."

Mum sighed. "Just be tolerant," she said. "Please."

We ate supper in the kitchen watching Twilight through the window. And we made plans, endless, impossible plans. Phantom was going to compete in horse shows all over Ireland. Angus was going to find his ideal horse and call it Tralee. We were going to grow fat on Kerry butter and milk fresh from the cow. I imagined a Georgian house at the end of a long drive, green fields fenced by banks, posts and rails; and horses everywhere of all shapes and sizes. And suddenly I didn't mind going any more.

"There will be turf fires," said Mum, "and Irish whiskey, which you are not to drink, and you'll go to the races I expect. And no one dresses up in Ireland, or hardly ever. You'll love it."

It was dark outside now, a warm dark night with no noise beside a gentle breeze stirring the leaves of the elms.

We talked for ages, all through the washing-up and afterwards drinking mugs of hot tea, because none of us felt like going to bed until at last Mum cried, "It's a quarter-past eleven. What are we thinking of? It's school tomorrow! Go to bed at once. Run. You'll never get up in the morning."

10

My room smelt of the roses in flower outside. It was a small friendly room with a bed, chest of drawers, and a table and chair and nothing much else. I had a row of china horses on my chest of drawers each named after a famous show-jumper, and a photograph of Phantom on my bedside table.

Lying in bed, I imagined us riding from dawn to dusk across green hills; Phantom growing fat and sleepy; a house full of foxes' masks, hunting whips and sporting prints. And now there was a moon which sent trickles of silvery light through my bedroom curtains and, I thought, Ireland may be beautiful but it can't be more beautiful than here. Then, without another thought I slept.

The next two weeks passed very quickly. Angus finished his exams. Mum bought clothes for Nigeria. We booked our tickets from London to Ireland. Mum arranged for Phantom to go by a horse-box which was to pick up three brood mares from a stud-farm near Dublin. The blossoms fell off the apple trees and lay like a pink carpet in the orchard. The longest day of the year came and went in a blaze of sunshine.

I didn't want to go to Ireland now. It was no good pretending any more. I wanted to jump Phantom at all the local shows, to try him in combined training competitions. I schooled him endlessly, circling him beneath the tall trees, halting and saluting an imagined judge, and Oxfordshire seemed the most beautiful place in the whole world.

Mum had her hair done and was ready to go, standing cool and immaculate in a lightweight uncrushable suit. In silence we waited for Aunt Nina to arrive. I couldn't speak, but Angus talked incessantly.

"We will write to you once a week," he said. "Don't

11

forget to buy me lots of postcards for my collection and bring me back some coins and stamps. You won't forget, will you?"

Aunt Nina had stopped outside now in her red sports car. As usual she was late. "Come on," she shrieked, "or we'll never make the airport."

She was wearing dark glasses and the latest fashion in hats, a silk dress and gloves. Angus and I climbed into the back of the car and put Mum's luggage on our knees. The lilac was coming out by the front gate and there was a squirrel running across the lawn.

"All set," cried Aunt Nina. "We're off."

She talked to Mum all the way to the airport about dull things like whether the sheets needed changing and where she could get her nails manicured. I had a knot in my stomach because Mum was going and I thought, supposing Phantom won't load, or Cousin Mary hates us?

The road was up outside the airport and we got caught in a long line of cars.

"Dad has left thirty pounds for you. It's in the top corner of his desk. If you need any more, ask your Cousin Mary," Mum said turning round to smile at us.

"I'll see they remember. Don't worry," replied Aunt Nina, hooting loudly at a cigar-smoking business man in a Porsche who was trying to edge round us. And then we were at the airport, watching Mum check in her baggage.

"You will write, won't you?" I asked anxiously.

"I'll ring you when I arrive. Don't worry," Mum answered. Her gate number was being called already. There was no time to talk. Her luggage disappeared.

"Be good," she said. "And don't worry about us. Look after yourselves. We should be back in three weeks or four at the longest." She kissed us both, and Aunt Nina on the cheek. She went through the gate without looking back. I wiped a rush of tears off my face and we went outside into the sunshine again, feeling as though we had lost something which could never be replaced.

"I wish Dad would change his job," I said furiously. "The summer's ruined, absolutely ruined and it will never happen again. Next year I shall be too old for half the children's classes. It isn't fair. And Phantom's just beginning to go really well."

"There are more important things in the world than horses. Learn to play the piano, study a foreign language. Look where languages have got me," replied Aunt Nina smugly. "If I didn't know five languages I would still be in a typing pool, and your father would be earning half what he does now. We studied every morning all through the holidays."

"I don't care about money," I answered. "I would rather have Mum and Dad at home any day."

Outside the airport another traffic jam awaited us.

"I missed a party for this," complained Aunt Nina. "I was invited to the Romanian Embassy."

"The roads are empty in Ireland," observed Angus. "We'll be able to ride without fear, think of that, Jean, and Dad says I can choose myself a horse and when we come back Twilight will be quite big."

"And the summer will be over," I replied bleakly. "All the shows, the holidays . . . everything."

"There is summer in Ireland you know, and horse shows for that matter," replied Aunt Nina, "though I can't say it's my cup of tea. I like central heating and the latest of everything. Ireland is horses and dogs, hunting, shooting and fishing plus lots of Irish whiskey. Just right for you, Jean."

Later she sat on my bed talking. "Don't you brush your hair at night?" she asked. "Look, it's all tangled and

13

your pyjamas are missing a button. Tomorrow I shall buy you a nightie; something really feminine to take away with you, and a pair of fluffy bedroom slippers. She looked inside my clothes cupboard. "You've hardly any dresses either," she continued. "And nothing pretty. You must try and grow up, Jean. You can't be a little girl forever."

I couldn't explain how I felt—that childhood was like a long summer which I didn't want to end, that life was perfect as it was. Instead I said, "I feel comfortable in jeans and I like my two dresses, and anyway no one dresses up in Ireland, except in Dublin, or for hunt balls—and I don't expect to go to either."

Aunt Nina sighed. "Sleep well," she said. "And wake me with a nice cup of tea. I'm not at my best in the morning."

I could hear her talking to Angus next door in French. She kept saying, "Bon, bon, très bon." Then she said in English, "I don't know why your parents don't send you to France. Jean needs to grow up and you could do with some French conversation."

I fell asleep then and dreamed that Aunt Nina was looking at me. She said, "Grow up, wear false eyelashes," and then she fetched hers and they were the colour of Phantom's tail. She stuck them onto my eyelids and suddenly my neck started to grow. When I looked in the mirror I had become a giraffe.

2

I put the kettle on and gazed at Twilight who was lying down beside Moonlight looking like a cuddly toy. I have always been able to get up early. I feel alive and full of energy the moment I awake, unlike Angus who is forever going back to sleep after the alarm clock has gone off. It was a lovely morning. The dew still lay on the grass, soaking my feet through my trainers. The cuckoo was calling "Cuckoo", Apple trees were joined by cobwebs, which vanished as the sun grew stronger and dried the dew. The garden smelt of lilac. Poor Mum in Nigeria, I thought, imagining blistering heat and a treeless landscape.

Aunt Nina was still asleep when I knocked on her bedroom door. Her room smelt of perfume. I put a mug of tea on the table beside the bed and touched her shoulder.

"Not a mug next time," she muttered opening her eyes. "A nice cup and saucer and lumps of sugar in a basin, and cream. Try and be dainty, Jean."

I tiptoed from the room without answering and screamed at Angus to get up. "You'll be late for school if you don't," I shouted, "and you've got a careers talk this morning."

I rode Phantom in the evening. Then Aunt Nina washed my hair and swamped it in the most disgusting setting lotion. Angus read about careers until he felt dizzy.

When my hair was dry I cooked the supper, while Aunt Nina lay on a towel on the lawn.

"I'm missing my little flat already," she said coming into the supper. "I like to hear London going on outside. Nothing happens here."

"There's lots going on if you know where to look," I replied quickly. "There's slugs eating the strawberries, and caterpillars on the cabbages, the peas are growing fatter in their pods and Phantom is learning to stand still while I count to twenty."

"And Twilight is growing bigger every second," interrupted my brother.

"The apples are growing on the trees, and over at the farm the cat is having kittens," I continued.

"And my mind is swallowing a huge quantity of facts about careers," added Angus.

"And listen, there's a car going by."

But Aunt Nina had her hands over her ears by this time. "Serve my food, Jean," she cried. "No, not like that . . . daintily. And not so much potato; I have to think of my figure."

She took her hands off her ears and continued, "I'm sorry for Cousin Mary, as your mother calls her, having to put up with you two for all those weeks. Three days is enough for me."

The next evening we took Mermaid, Moonlight and Twilight to the farm, leaving Phantom behind in the stable. Twilight trotted along behind her mother looking sweet. The farmer, Mr Barnes, said, "Don't you worry, I'll look after the foal. I've had horses all my life. I'll see she won't come to no harm. So enjoy yourselves in Ireland."

We turned the ponies into a forty-acre field just as the sun was going down.

"We are terribly grateful," said my brother politely. "We really don't know what we would do without you."

Walking homewards, we discussed Aunt Nina. "She was furious because I spilt oats in my bedroom," I said.

"She's so fussy. Never mind, only two more days. Phantom goes tomorrow, doesn't he?" asked Angus.

When we got home we found a message from Mum saying ARRIVED SAFELY. LOVE MUM ... nothing more. "I suppose Mum will write to us at Cousin Mary's," I suggested. "Perhaps we'll find a letter when we get there." I was missing her all the time now, whereas Angus insisted that he was quite capable on his own. "If Aunt Nina wasn't with us, I would be perfectly happy," he said. The weather had changed while we walked. The sky had darkened, an ominous breeze stirred the trees. The air was so close that one felt trapped. Phantom was stamping in the stable. The flies had retreated to the safety of hedges. Everything seemed to be waiting for the storm to break. I gave Phantom some hay and filled up his water bucket. "You can stay in tonight," I said. "And tomorrow I'll get up early and ride you. Then in the evening you will go away in a box and we'll meet you again in Ireland." Suddenly the future seemed immensely exciting, waiting like a book to be read. As I went inside the storm broke. Great jagged flashes of lightening lit the sky. The thunder was deafening when it came. Aunt Nina sat with her hands over her ears wishing herself back in London. "Only one more day in the country," she gasped. "I'm a Londoner through and through. Eat your supper for goodness sake. I can't eat a thing while the storm lasts." She was wearing a pyjama suit, a long

17

necklace—which reached to her waist—and lots of perfume.

"We are sorry you had to come. Personally, I think we are old enough to look after ourselves. Unfortunately our parents thought otherwise," said Angus in a dignified voice.

"Take your shoes off. Can't you see I've washed the floor?" continued Aunt Nina as though Angus had never spoken. "Honestly, you children, you're only half civilised."

"We are not children," replied Angus.

I rose at dawn the next morning; all the birds were singing. It was better than any chorus I had ever heard before. Don't their throats ever get tired? I wondered, putting on Phantom's saddle. The sun was coming up beyond the beech woods. Everything still sparkled after the thunderstorm. One could almost feel things growing. I saw that the roses were coming out around the front porch as I swung into the saddle. The roads were empty. We seemed to have the whole world to ourselves, except for the creak of the saddle and the eternal bird-song. I rode through the woods where everything smelt of damp earth and wet leaves, and remembered the places I had ridden before—the Blue Ridge Mountains of Virginia, lovely too, but in a completely different way. I wanted my ride to last forever; but all too soon the sun was up, drying the leaves, the post van passed along the road and in the distance I heard the chink of milk bottles.

I cantered back through the woods and now the sun made patterns through the leaves; the bird-song was hushed, men in caps passed on bicycles. Oh, for life to be like this for ever, I thought, turning down the twisty road to home. But no, one must grow up, go out into the world, work and be educated, worry over gas bills and the washing-up, and whether the floor's clean.

I put Phantom back in the stable, untacked and groomed him quickly with a body brush; then I bandaged his tail, fetched him clean water, mixed him a feed and filled his hay net. It was really morning now. A boy pushed a paper through our letter-box, the flowers opened their petals, the sun moved so that it shone directly on Sparrow Cottage. I made tea for Aunt Nina and poured it into a best cup and saucer and took it upstairs on a tray, leaving my shoes in the hall. Then I wakened Angus.

"This is our last day," I said. "We'll have to pack tonight; so for goodness sake get up." And all the time there was a well of sadness inside me because we were leaving, and battling against it a rising tide of excitement. I imagined a splendid house, set in a quiet landscape, incessant talk of horses, a cousin who was a kindred spirit. I ran downstairs whistling. The post had come. I picked up the letters, but there was nothing for me or Angus.

School seemed a waste of time, for how could geometry matter when tomorrow I would be in Ireland, when Phantom might not load in the evening, when life suddenly seemed so intensely exciting? History seemed irrelevant to my mood; for who could care about the past when the future waited like a mountain to be climbed?

School was over at last. I caught the bus with Angus who was worrying about his exams again. "What is the meaning of clandestine?" he asked.

"Secret, not mentioned, hidden, I suppose," I answered.

"I didn't put that," wailed Angus. "I put something else. I bet I've failed. Dad will be furious."

Everybody shrieked after us when we left the bus.

"Have a good time, bring us back some shamrock. Bring stamps, coins . . . have a good time . . ." Their voices were drowned by the sound of the engine starting up again. I felt as though I was about to begin a new life. "Tomorrow we will be gone," I said to the road. "We won't walk on you any more."

"You're mad," said Angus. "Why do you talk such nonsense? I'm suddenly certain I've failed English, I know I have." His face looked pale in the sunlight.

"What nonsense!"

"Talking to the road as though it was a person," he shouted.

"The horse-box is coming at five," I said, starting to run. But when I reached home the loose box was empty. I felt my heart leap . . . He's gone, he's got out, I thought, running towards the cottage, shrieking, "Phantom's gone, Aunt Nina. Phantom's gone."

She was lying on the lawn in a bikini. "Of course he has, they came early. Good thing too, considering what he was like to box; they were here for two hours."

I felt let down. I had wanted to box Phantom myself, to say goodbye to him.

"Oh I see," I said. "But he would have boxed all right for me."

"Tea's on the table; and you had better start packing. By the way, I've got you a present."

Aunt Nina picked up a bottle of tanning lotion and came inside with us. "I went into Henley and got it for you."

She handed me a parcel which contained a pink nightie with frills and a pair of fluffy bedroom slippers. I said, "Thank you, you are kind," thinking of all the things I would much rather have been given—a new pair of jodhpurs, a new riding hat, a set of leg bandages for Phantom. I shan't wear it, I thought. I hate frills.

Angus and I stuffed things into our cases. We kept

weighing them on the bathroom scales and then taking things out again.

"It's your riding boots and hat which are so heavy, can't you leave them behind?" asked Aunt Nina, leaning over us.

We shook our heads. I longed to take out the frilly nightie, but I couldn't with Aunt Nina watching.

"Take a dress instead of jeans. Haven't you something in nylon or crimplene," asked Aunt Nina going to my wardrobe. "That hardly weighs a thing."

In the end we put our jodhpur boots and riding hats in a duffle bag which Angus said he would carry as hand luggage. Then we shut and locked our cases. I wandered out to the stable, mucked it out and listened to hens cackling in the distance and the whirr of a machine turning the last of the hay on the farm. Tomorrow we would be in Ireland; it seemed impossible. Supposing we hate Cousin Mary? Angus thinks he's so capable, but he isn't really. He's reckless and he says aggravating things. And suddenly, standing in the peaceful English twilight, I was filled with apprehension and doubts. I saw Angus arguing with Irishmen. I imagined Cousin Mary saying, "I think it would be better if you left immediately." And where would we go? Little did I know then what really lay in wait for us. Perhaps if I had known I would have begged Aunt Nina to stay. I would have cabled Mum COME BACK. I would have missed the plane on purpose. Instead I wandered indoors and ate a cold supper with Aunt Nina and Angus in the kitchen, discussing boring subjects like motor cars, the necessity of speaking good French and whether Paris fashion still leads the world.

3

England lay below us, a patchwork of fields dotted with houses like a model village. We read the directions provided for us, and checked that our life-jackets were under our seats.

There was nothing but clouds outside now and an occasional patch of blue. The captain made an announcement which we couldn't hear. Coffee and fruit juices were served. Someone said, "I can see land below. It's Ireland."

I had bubbles in my ears. Presently we were going down, our safety-belts fastened. Below were fields; then the buildings of the airport. It was a long run in and there was a small jolt as we taxied onto the ground. We unfastened our safety-belts. In a moment we would meet Cousin Mary. What was she like I wondered, and what about her daughter? Would we enjoy ourselves? Or would the whole holidays be a misery, so much wasted time?

Everyone was leaving the plane. Outside, the sun was shining as we followed each other onto a bus, like sheep.

"Cousin Mary is going to meet us on the other side of the Customs. And I've still got the thirty pounds," said Angus feeling his breast pocket. He was wearing corduroys and a hacking jacket. Aunt Nina had made me wear a skirt and jumper. I felt ridiculous in them— as if I was returning to my old school instead of embarking on three weeks of adventure in Ireland, for that is how I saw it even then, and as things turned out, I was right.

We waited ages for our luggage by a sort of round-about which had a conveyor belt attached, so that when the suitcases arrived one just leaned down and picked them up as they went past.

"I hope Phantom's all right," I said. "It's awful not knowing where he is."

"He probably spent the night in the horse-box on the boat. He may be there before us," replied Angus. "Look, there's your suitcase. Grab it."

"What are you here for?" asked the Customs official.

"For a visit," answered my brother, and suddenly I saw for the first time how tall he had become.

"I hope you enjoy it." He chalked our bags and then we were past him, our eyes searching for Cousin Mary. Our luggage had been a long time arriving so that nearly all the other passengers had already left. Cousin Mary stood with a girl of about my age. They both wore droopy skirts and cardigans. They pointed and looked at one another, when they saw us.

"She's awfully wispy," said Angus quickly, "and her mouth turns down at the corners."

She was the opposite of Aunt Nina, and since we had criticised Aunt Nina so much to each other we probably deserved the opposite. Aunt Nina seemed on top of the world most of the time and always afraid she was missing something. One glance at Cousin Mary told us that the world had defeated her.

Angus smiled and held out his hand. "Hi, I'm Angus," he said. We shook hands.

"Has Phantom arrived?" I asked, picking up my case again.

"Phantom?"

"My horse."

23

"Not yet, I think," replied Cousin Mary. "He will be going straight to O'Reagan's when he does. We don't have the farm any more. O'Reagan is very good with horses." She had a lilt to her voice.

Angus was introducing himself to our cousin, Fiona, as we walked outside into the sunshine.

"Wait here and I'll bring the car round," said Cousin Mary.

"Why do you have to bring a horse? O'Reagan has an awful lot of horses."

"If I left him at home or on the farm he would jump out and disappear," I answered, noting her low, broad forehead, her blue eyes and long dark hair pushed behind pointed ears.

"He came from America. He was wild in the Blue Ridge Mountains. I caught him and tamed him but I'm always afraid he'll go wild again," I continued.

"O'Reagan understands horses. He'll look after him well for sure," said Fiona.

Cousin Mary tooted her horn. We loaded our cases into the car. There wasn't much room when we were all inside.

"Welcome to Eire," said Cousin Mary. "I've grown to love it. I hope you will too."

Dublin seemed to go on for ever, but at last we reached the country. "We will stop in a minute and have a bite to eat," said Cousin Mary.

"It's just like England," replied Angus sounding disappointed.

"It's different where we live," replied Fiona. "It's awful wild and very beautiful, isn't it, Mother?"

"Too wild. We only have turf fires, though we have the electricity and the telephone when it isn't cut off," replied Cousin Mary.

"Is it good riding country?" I wanted to know.

"You will find it awful wild at first, but better when you know it," replied Fiona.

"She doesn't ride," said Cousin Mary, stopping the car in a lay-by. "She never took to it."

"Are the fences high?" I asked, stepping out into the soft Irish air, staring at the blooming gorse which was everywhere.

"Why on earth?" asked Cousin Mary.

"Because Phantom jumps out," I said.

"Oh, they're high, awful high," replied Fiona. "Mr O'Reagan keeps them high. He's a wonderful man, Mr O'Reagan, a truly wonderful man. You won't have any trouble with Mr O'Reagan around, will she mother?"

Cousin Mary laughed. "Fiona has great faith in Donnie O'Reagan," she said. "But he *is* good with horses. It's his trade you know."

We ate ham sandwiches while Angus made polite conversation and the sky clouded over. A caravan went by drawn by a piebald horse. Cars were few and far between.

We drove on and the countryside grew wilder; once we saw the sea, a cold grey sea with gorse reaching right down to it and never a boat or a person to be seen. Sheep grazed by the roadside now. They had the long wool used for Arran sweaters and small black faces. The ground looked wet and boggy and everywhere there was turf cutting going on. We passed solitary ruined towers and once the remains of a magnificent castle.

"We are nearly there," said Cousin Mary.

I looked for houses but saw nothing but moors reaching up to where gorse and rock met the grey sky. A donkey cart went by with two curly-headed boys laughing in it. Men in dark suits pedalled bicycles. An old woman rode sideways on the back of a donkey. We

25

passed a bungalow fenced round by a high stone wall, with black heifers grazing under the windows.

"It's beautiful," my brother exclaimed. "Fantastic. Look at the boulders."

The fields were fenced by boulders—crazy, crooked tumbling fields, yellow with gorse and grey with boulders. I wanted to laugh but I couldn't, for I kept thinking, how will Phantom fit in here? Will he have to be stabled all the time? What will he eat?

"I'm so glad you've come. It's years since we had visitors," said Cousin Mary, turning round to smile at us. "You'll be very welcome and so will your horse, Jean, spare no thought for him. He will be in clover."

But there was no clover. There had been lush green fields outside Dublin, with the hay newly carried and fat cows grazing to their heart's content; there had been racecourses and mares and foals—plump and contented—standing under beautiful trees. But here, instead of hay there were cones of peat drying on the moors and nothing except the bleating of sheep and the faint clip-clop of wild donkeys' hoofs to be heard. It was wilder than the Blue Ridge Mountains of Virginia. It made me think of the beginning of the world. I expected dinosaurs to appear from behind boulders. The houses were built of stone with only one storey. I felt that they had stood there for centuries.

"This is just a small part of Ireland. It isn't all like this," said Cousin Mary.

I could see ponies grazing in a field. The sky was blue again now. It looked marvellous against the vivid yellow gorse. We turned a corner and there before us lay a lake with wooded hills beyond, too beautiful for words to describe.

"Tourists come here for the fishing," said Cousin Mary.

But there was no one there; just a few boats lying on the shore.

"Only a few more miles now," said Fiona. The hills were flattening out. There were tracks through gentle valleys and fewer boulders. A tower stood in the distance completely alone. We passed a cluster of cottages and a shop. "What paradise," exclaimed my brother. "I wish we lived here. Not just occassionally but all the time."

"You would too. It's a beautiful place, surely it is," replied Fiona.

I could feel my heart thudding against my ribs with excitement. The road dipped downwards now; low mountains lay around us like sleeping giants. The ground was drier; there were no turf cutters here. I could see horses grazing in a field. Beyond the field stood an incongruous grey house, looking naked against the hills.

"That's home," said Fiona. "And you're very welcome, I'll be telling you. And that's Mr O'Reagan's cottage," she said presently, pointing at a low building at the beginning of the drive. "If your horse has arrived he will be caring for it, Jean, have no fear."

I was gripping the seats now, trying to imagine weeks and weeks in the unwelcoming grey house.

"It's a fine place," said Fiona. "Everyone says so; and there's history about it too. Have you warned them about the attics, Mother? You had better be telling them for sure."

"You mustn't go in them. The floors are not safe," explained Cousin Mary. "Last year a young boy went up and fell through the ceiling and broke his leg."

"It was a terrible business," said Fiona. "He was crying and crying and no one heard him. So please understand, you mustn't go up there, isn't that so, Mother?"

27

"I've just said so," replied Cousin Mary.

We stepped out of the car. The garden was over-grown. The paint was peeling off the front door. Two rough collie dogs greeted us with smiles and licks. The air smelt fresh and a breeze stirred the gorse on the hills.

"It's fabulous," cried Angus, taking great gulps of air. "I'm so glad we've come."

The hall floor was covered with brown linoleum. Everything was comfortably shabby, the carpets, the chair covers, the curtains.

"You are on the first floor," announced Cousin Mary.

"I will be showing you your rooms," said Fiona.

As I followed her upstairs, I wished that I could reach her somehow through her Irishness. I had an awful feeling that I was never to know her properly.

My room looked at the hills. Clean home-washed sheets lay in a heap on the bed; the window was open. It was a big room with an armchair and an enormous cupboard, a table covered by a cloth, an ancient chair and a gigantic mirror. Someone had put a vase of flowers on the table.

"It is a beautiful room," said Fiona. "Now I must show you the stairs to the attic. They are very unsafe. They will break if you step on them, truly they will and the attic door is locked." She seemed possessed by the stairs though they appeared ordinary enough, just a single wooden flight leading to a door.

"OK, I'm warned," I said. "Thank you for everything."

"And the bathroom, you'll be wanting to see the bathroom."

I expected a wooden bath but it was quite modern and looked towards Donnie O'Reagan's cottage.

"That will be all right then," she said with a brief smile. "Tea will be ready very soon."

I returned to my room and wondered where Phantom was and why our parents had not written. It was evening already, our first evening in Ireland. I wished that Phantom had arrived; I wanted to see him, to know that he was all right. I changed out of my skirt into jeans and a pullover and washed my face in the bathroom. I could see a square of buildings behind Donnie O'Reagan's cottage. They would be the stables, I decided.

Angus joined me in the passage. "It's tea," he said. "We are about to taste Irish soda bread for the first time. Isn't it super here? I shall be able to collect stones for my geology project and ride O'Reagan's horses. I'm so glad we came, aren't you? And Cousin Mary's nice, isn't she? Not like Aunt Nina. She won't buy you frilly nighties." He was laughing now, half dancing down the stairs. There seemed to be sunlight everywhere, shining through the passage windows and suddenly I felt happy too. "Phantom will like it here," I said. "It's so peaceful."

4

It was a high tea. The milk was straight from Donnie O'Reagan's cows, the butter was pale, home-made butter.

I kept listening for the sound of a horse-box. "Phantom should be here by now," I said. "He left yesterday."

"Be patient," replied Cousin Mary.

After tea we wandered along the rough drive to Donnie O'Reagan's cottage. Fiona knocked on the cottage door.

A woman opened the door. She was holding a child in her arms with three more standing behind her, all small and grubby.

"Is it Donnie you will be wanting?" she inquired. "He's down at the village just now."

"These are my relations from England," Fiona said. "Will he be long?"

"An hour, but you're welcome." Mrs O'Reagan smiled at us while a child started to scream in the background.

"Can we look round the horses, please?" I asked. "And has mine arrived by any chance? He's a golden palomino."

She shook her head. "Go and look at Donnie's horses though, you're welcome," she added.

The stable reminded me of Virginia. The loose boxes

were inside, each walled by concrete with a wooden door; there were windows at the back of the stable and the horses could look out through them. The floors were covered with peat.

"He's brought them in because of the flies; he'll put them out when he returns home," Fiona said.

There were only four, a big bay with a blaze and two white socks behind, an iron grey which was only three, a chestnut called Sunrise and a piebald of about fifteen-two.

"He has some ponies outside," Fiona told us. "I don't know their names but Mr O'Reagan is real fond of them all; they are like children to him."

"If only Phantom would arrive," I said. "I can't help worrying." Now the hills were shrouded in mist. The house looked greyer than ever when we returned to it. Only a few windows were curtained; most of them blazed light into the gathering dusk.

"Have you lived here long?" my brother asked.

"All my life except when I'm at school. I did go to the National school, but now I attend a convent. It is truly marvellous," Fiona made 'marvellous' sound like something out of this world. "I am going to be a nun," she continued, "like dear Sister Teresa. She is hardly on this earth. She is a saintly woman if ever there was one."

"How can you be a nun?" I asked after a short silence. "You'll have to give up so much."

"But I will be like Sister Teresa; I will be at peace," she said.

There were mugs of hot chocolate and biscuits waiting for us in the kitchen. "Can't I stay up till Phantom comes?" I asked.

"O'Reagan will attend to him," replied Cousin Mary.

"But he's out . . ."

"You have had a long day. You must go to bed

31

soon," replied Cousin Mary in a determined voice. "I have made up your beds and put hot water-bottles in them. I hope you sleep well."

It was eight-thirty. The whole valley was covered in mist. Fiona's going to be a nun, I thought, but perhaps it will suit her; she is certainly peculiar enough. I opened my bedroom window and leaned out. I could see the pebbly drive below, nothing more. And Phantom hasn't come. I shall never sleep, I thought. I can't when he's missing. What will we do if he never turns up? Why didn't Mum give us more details of his arrangements? This place must be miles from any stud-farm. I could hear my brother singing next door as I pulled the ancient wooden shutters across my window, undressed, put on pyjamas and climbed into bed.

I don't know how long I had been asleep when I heard someone banging on a door. At first it was just part of a dream, then I knew it was real. I thought I was still at home and for an awful moment I could find neither the light switch nor the door. I fell over the Jacobean chair, bruising my shin before I realised the truth. Then I put on the light, opened the shutters and looked out into almost utter darkness. A voice called, "I've brought the horse. I couldn't make O'Reagan hear. Where shall I put him?"

"Hang on. I'll be down in a minute," I shouted. "He's my horse." I could see the dim outline of a Land Rover and a trailer with a head staring over the top. When Phantom heard my voice he whinnied. I put on wellington boots and an anorak over my pyjamas, switched on a passage light and ran downstairs. The front door was bolted, barred and chained. It was ages before I could open it. Outside there was a fog, what Dad would have called "a real pea-souper". A man wearing a cap stood with a flashlight. "It took us all morning to load him. You'll have to back him out," he said.

Phantom gave a low whinny. A light went on in O'Reagan's cottage. We let down the ramp and I backed Phantom out slowly on to the gravel drive.

"I'll take him to the stable. Could you bring your light?" I asked. Phantom was covered with dry sweat and shivering in the night air.

"He wouldn't eat a thing," the man said.

I put Phantom in an empty box and fetched him hay and water.

"It's twenty pounds you'll be owing me and I'd like you to settle up now if you don't mind. It was a terrible long way on a night like this," the man said.

"Twenty pounds!" I exclaimed. I'll have to wake up Angus, and it will leave us with only ten pounds in the world, I thought.

"I'll wait here," said the man. "But I'd be glad if you'd be quick. It's a long time I've been on the road."

I ran upstairs in my boots and knocked on Angus's door. He didn't answer so I went in and shook him, shouting, "Wake up, Phantom's come and I've got to have twenty pounds."

"Twenty pounds?" exclaimed Angus at last. "That's a lot of money."

"Where is it? The man's waiting outside. I can't think why you didn't wake up. He must have been banging on the door for ages," I said.

"In the breast pocket of my jacket. It's in fivers."

I grabbed four fivers and ran downstairs again. As I ran I could have sworn a light went out in the attic. I slammed the front door after me. Mr O'Reagan had appeared by this time. "I'll fetch your horse a rug," he said. "He's awful cold."

I handed the driver the four fivers. Angus was standing beside me now, saying, "I think there's someone in the attic! Do you think we had better wake up Cousin Mary?"

But now I could only worry about Phantom. "He's shivering, he may get pneumonia," I said.

"Who's he?" asked my brother stupidly.

"Phantom of course." Mr O'Reagan had hung a lantern in the stable. He rubbed Phantom down and rugged him up. "He's a grand little horse," he said. "Now you slip back to bed. He'll be all right in the morning. He's just awful cold from the journey, and it'll be you who'll be getting pneumonia in a minute."

Angus stood beside me with chattering teeth. "The light keeps going on and off," he said, "it's most mysterious."

"It's nothing," I answered. "It can't be, you know what Fiona said."

"Exactly."

My teeth were chattering too by this time. It was as though the fog had reached the marrow of my bones. I did not want to think about the attic. I just wanted to go back to bed and sleep.

"There isn't a light now," I said. "Look. We've just imagined it because we're tired. I'm going back to bed." I was too cold to run. Angus followed in silence. "I'll lock up," he said. "I don't know why Cousin Mary isn't awake; you made enough noise. The whole house shook when you slammed the front door."

"She must be a sound sleeper."

"And Fiona too."

I helped him shoot the bolts. "I shall have to look in the attic sometime," he continued, following me upstairs. "There's something going on."

"Phantom's arrived, isn't that enough without inventing mysteries?" I replied.

"I haven't invented anything," Angus answered. "There *was* someone in the attic."

34

"A ghost," I said, "Good-night." I was too tired to be afraid of ghosts. I tried to stay awake. I strained my ears hoping to hear footsteps, but almost at once I fell asleep to dream that I was riding Phantom in a show.

The next thing I knew was Fiona shaking me. She was wearing a pinny and smelt of kitchen soap. The sun was streaming through the window.

"It's breakfast," she said. "It's past nine o'clock."

"I'm sorry," I answered, sitting up. "Phantom arrived in the night."

"I know. I heard everything."

I wanted to say, "Even the noise in the attic?" but I didn't. Angus will be telling everyone soon enough, I thought. And we will look silly if it's rats or mice.

I dressed quickly. I wanted to see Phantom, but Cousin Mary was waiting by the breakfast table. My brother was eating porridge.

"Phantom's arrived," I said.

"So I heard. Did you sleep well?"

"Yes, thank you."

Fiona insisted on waiting on us. It embarrassed me, but Angus seemed happy enough with the arrangement. It was a perfect morning for a ride, and I wanted to be out on the hills before the weather changed.

"Did you hear any noises last night?" Angus asked, buttering soda bread. "I mean besides the trailer."

"Surely. I heard your sister going down the stairs and the door opening," Fiona replied. "But mother takes sleeping pills; she hears nothing."

"I heard lots of strange noises," said my brother thoughtfully.

"It must have been the mice then. We have an awful lot of mice," replied Fiona quickly.

"In the attic? That explains everything," replied my brother, but he didn't sound convinced.

"And rats, too, a terrible lot of rats."

"We need a cat," said Cousin Mary. "We must ask the O'Reagans for a kitten."

But rats don't switch on lights, I thought suddenly; so there *is* a mystery, and now Angus will never leave it alone. He willl be like a hound on the scent of something, running here, running there with his nose to the ground, when all I want is peace and a chance to school Phantom.

"There's the postman," said Cousin Mary, and collected half a dozen letters off the mat in the hall. "One for each of you," she said, sorting through them, "and all the rest are bills."

Mine was from Mum. She said that they were all right, but that they envied us the peace and quiet of Ireland. *The heat is tremendous,* she wrote, *and the people wear very bright clothes! I hope Phantom has turned up and is in good shape. Help Cousin Mary and try to be friends with Fiona, who is by all accounts a lonely and reserved child.* There followed a whole page about the people she had met. Then she sent love from them both.

"Mine is from Dad," said Angus. "He hasn't been kidnapped yet."

"Swop," I suggested holding out my letter.

Cousin Mary watched us with the envy of someone who never gets a letter. I wanted to say, "I'll write to you every week when I get home." But suddenly home seemed very far away, almost like another world.

We didn't pass our letters to Cousin Mary to read. I thought they were too personal and it never occurred to Angus. I put my dirty breakfast things in the kitchen sink. "Can we wash up?" I offered.

Cousin Mary shook her head. "I've got nothing else to do this morning, but you can make your beds. Fiona will help."

Fiona was an expert bed maker. She did not think much of my efforts.

"You have not tucked in your corners," she observed. "And the bottom sheet will come adrift, truly it will."

"I don't mind. I'm a good sleeper. I don't notice creases," I said.

"Now we will be making your brother's bed," she said.

"Can't he make his own? He always does at home," I said, my heart aching to see Phantom.

"Boys can't make beds," sniffed Fiona.

Angus had pulled his together and opened his window, but he had forgotten his pyjamas which lay in a heap on the floor. Fiona sniffed and took the bed to pieces, while I stood sullenly by, thinking, I'm not going through this every morning. But at last I was outside running down the drive. I found Angus talking to Donnie O'Reagan. "You have been an age," he said. "I'm going to ride the piebald. He's called Peppermint."

"It isn't fair. I had to help Fiona make beds."

"I made mine."

"She remade it."

"She's a grand girl," said Donnie O'Reagan.

Phantom was warm and dry. He nuzzled my pockets and licked my hand.

"I'll take him out," I said. "Otherwise he'll go mad staying in all the time. He jumps out of fields," I explained. "I don't think your walls will keep him in if he had the mind to go."

Angus was tacking up Peppermint with an ancient saddle which needed a blanket under it. The snaffle bit was thin and twisted and there was a running martingale as well.

Donnie O'Reagan fetched Phantom's tack from the saddle room. "It nearly went back with Mr O'Brien," he said. "It was lucky I saw it. He's a grand little horse though."

"He came from America."

"Did he now?" replied Mr O'Reagan who started to tell us of his relatives on the other side of the Atlantic. "They've done well, very well for themselves," he said. "They're rich men now."

Angus mounted Peppermint while Mr O'Reagan held his stirrup. "Keep to the path now," he told us. "There's bogs in the hills and it is easy enough to be lost."

"Isn't this marvellous?" I asked Angus as we rode away from the stables, "We are really in Ireland, Phantom's arrived and we are actually riding."

"What did you expect to happen?" asked Angus. "I thought we came here to ride."

"Yes, I know. But it still seems fantastic," I answered, looking at the hills which had seen so much and changed so little in a thousand years.

"I'm going to gather rocks and stones and there's marble in these hills, too," Angus said. "*And* I'm going to explore the attic."

"Oh, for goodness sake mind your own business. There may be anything in there."

"Such as . . . ?"

"Stolen property," I answered.

"Exactly," replied Angus in a cool voice. "Or something even worse."

"Do shut up," I said. "I want to enjoy my holiday."

"It was you who said stolen property," replied my brother.

"I didn't mean to. Do you like Peppermint? He's got a lovely long stride, longer than Phantom's. And I love his odd-coloured hoofs."

"Yes," replied Angus starting to trot. "And he knows these hills, which may be useful, for it must be easy to get lost if a fog comes down."

Phantom danced along. His hoofs hardly seemed to touch the ground. His head was high, his ears pricked. "He must have hated the trailer journey. There was no roof and he had to look out over the top through iron bars," I said.

"Fiona knows what goes on in the attic," my brother remarked. "You can see it in her face. She's sly, terribly sly. That's why she doesn't want us to know her properly. She's afraid of what we might find out."

"How can you be so awful when she's going to be a nun?" I answered. "Come on, let's canter."

There were curlews, the smell of damp peaty earth and the sun suddenly warm on our backs. I wanted the morning to last for ever; but already there were clouds gathering on the horizon and I had a sense of approaching doom as we turned homewards. Phantom stretched his neck and tried to outwalk Peppermint, and my brother hardly spoke.

After a time I could bear his silence no longer. "There must be some perfectly simple explanation," I said. "Perhaps Donnie O'Reagan keeps his oats in the attic and was fetching some."

"At midnight? Anyway, we would have seen him."

"He might have sent someone else."

"Who? Honestly, you're pathetic."

"And you're crime mad," I shouted, pushing Phantom into a trot. "You want to discover something awful so that you can have your name in the newspaper. You just want something cheap and sensational like: 'English Boy Solves Irish Crime', that's the sort of headline you're after. And you're spoiling our holiday. Look at the view. It's fantastic, but you haven't even noticed it because all you can think of is noises in the attic . . ."

I was cantering away from him now with the wind in my face touched by the first drops of rain. "I love it here," I cried. "I want to be happy. I want to get on with Fiona, to be friends; but you are spoiling everything."

5

In the afternoon Cousin Mary packed a picnic and took us to see a lake. The clouds had cleared; the water reflected wooden hills and the pebbly shore was completely deserted. Angus collected specimens of rock. "I am going to read Geology at University," he explained. "And then get a job in Australia. I don't want to stay in England, it's too overcrowded. In fifty years there won't be any proper country left."

"There will still be country in Eire," Cousin Mary replied. "What do you plan to do when you're grown-up, Jean?"

"School horses," I replied. "Break and make, and deal a bit too. I may teach riding as well. I shall have to start in a small way though, because I haven't any capital."

I looked at Fiona and imagined her dressed as a nun, walking in a rose garden behind a high wall, saying her rosary. It was impossible to tell what she was thinking. Her face was like a shuttered window—one couldn't tell what went on inside. I longed to wrench open the shutters, to know what really lay beyond.

The midges were biting now and a haze lay over the lake. We packed up the picnic things.

"It's a fabulous place," I said. "I would like to live here with a boat and catch my own fish for supper, and ride and never have a car."

We climbed into Cousin Mary's car and all the time I felt as though we were buying time, that the peace wouldn't last, that soon, quite soon Angus would find out something and the storm would break.

The road was almost empty. Cousin Mary gave an old lady a lift to the next town. When she got out she blessed us all repeatedly. "God bless you, Madam," she cried. "And your children. God be with you always, Madam. Thank you, and God bless you all; may you grow up strong and healthy."

We could see the house now, grey in the distance, and the tower on the hill beyond.

"It's been a lovely day," I said. "I really do love it here. I'm so glad we came." A man in a suit cycled slowly along the road and everywhere the turf cutters were going home.

"We will go somewhere else tomorrow, but the next day I have to go to Dublin with Fiona," said Cousin Mary. "She has to have new clothes for school next term, and she has no summer dresses. She will be needing some shoes as well. And I want to get my hair done. It will be rather dull for you two. You will be following us round, bored to death no doubt."

I could feel my brother's mind working so that before he spoke I knew already what he would say. "Can we stay behind? We'll be very sensible. After all I *am* fifteen. Lots of people are starting work at that age."

"Well, Mrs O'Flatery will be coming in the morning. She could leave you some lunch. I'll think about it," replied Cousin Mary.

And I could feel my brother's excitement growing as he sat beside me in the car. I knew he was imagining himself in the attics—discovering what? Starting what chain of reaction? I was afraid he would begin something we couldn't stop. I looked at the darkly dressed figures going home along the quiet road. Outwardly they were friendly enough; but what did they think about as they walked or cycled? And what about the youths racing past us now in a donkey cart? The signposts were in Gaelic, the English words underneath had been painted out.

"Do you know Irish?" I asked Cousin Mary.

"You mean the Gaelic?" she asked and shook her head. "But Fiona's learning it—you have to have it nowadays if you want to go into the Civil Service or be a nurse. They won't take you otherwise."

She was talking more like us. It was as though she had lapsed back into her old English ways because we were there.

"I should like to learn Gaelic," I said. "Then I might understand the signposts."

"Fiona will teach you," replied Cousin Mary. "Won't you, dear?"

Fiona nodded noncommittally and now we were home. The dogs met us with joyous faces. "I must see Phantom. He gets bored with being in all day," I cried.

He was looking out of his window, golden and unreal, like a magic horse; something which would appear today from nowhere and be gone tomorrow. I talked to him for a long time and then Donnie O'Reagan came. He was a small man with greying hair who moved very quietly, though he talked enough. We compared the price of hay and sets of shoes, and he told me again of his relations across the sea—there seemed all the time in the world just then. "So they'll be going to Dublin," he said presently nodding towards the big house.

"Yes, but Angus and I are staying. We're not keen on towns and it's so lovely here. I don't want to miss a minute of it."

Donnie O'Reagan looked pleased. He patted me on the back and said that I was a "right good lass", and we started to talk about schooling horses and how to

43

teach a horse to jump banks; and over everything hung the wonderful smell of horse, of saddle soap and new-made hay.

At last Angus called, "Supper, hurry up. Everybody's waiting."

I patted Phantom and said goodbye to Donnie O'Reagan and felt bewitched by the peace of Ireland, so that suddenly I wanted to stay for ever.

Supper was soon eaten and after we had washed-up Angus followed me into my bedroom.

"I've found the key to the attic," he whispered, shutting my door. "It was hanging up in the cupboard under the stairs." He held out a key with a luggage label on it. "Read it," he said triumphantly.

"I don't want to," I replied. "We were asked to stay out of the attics by our hosts. I think it's bad manners to go in."

"You are afraid of what you may find. I'll go alone; then *you* won't upset anyone."

"Supposing we fall through the floor?" I asked next.

"We will be extra careful," replied my brother. I saw that his eyes were lit up with excitement.

"I hope we don't find anything," I said, and Angus smiled because he knew now that I was going with him.

"I'll wake you up around midnight," he said. "Put trainers on. We won't need a torch." He skipped out of my room while I stood looking at the hills, wondering where Mum was at this moment and whether she was missing us. I could hear a donkey braying and from somewhere the sound of running water. In the distance a thin grey streak of smoke floated up into the night sky. Below me, the garden was nothing but weeds; now in the approaching darkness it had a strange wild magic of its own. I washed and changed and climbed into bed wondering what the night held for us, and whether everything would be the same in the morning. And

44

gradually the lights went out all over the house. I lay thinking about Phantom, making plans for him, imagining the future. There seemed so much to look forward to: our parents coming home, hunter trials in the autumn, Twilight growing, Angus having a new horse. Outside the moon had risen now. I had left my shutters open and there was a moonbeam across the old Persian carpet which covered my bedroom floor. I shall school Phantom tomorrow, I decided, and look for something to jump; the stone walls shouldn't be too difficult.

It seemed but a moment later when I wakened to find Angus standing over me. "It's midnight," he said.

I clambered out of bed and found my trainers. I felt peevish and ready to quarrel over the least thing.

"I bet there's nothing there," I muttered. "And if there is, it's none of our business. Why must you meddle?"

But Angus ignored my grumbling. "Don't make a noise," he whispered, opening my bedroom door. "I hope the stairs won't creak."

The moon lit up the passage. Everything seemed unreal; my heart had started to pound against my ribs in an idiotic fashion, and I would have done anything to be back in bed fast asleep. But Angus had one foot on the stairs and he turned to give me an absurd, reckless, impish grin. To him it was just an escapade—nothing more. The stairs *did* creak; there was nothing we could do about it. I felt inexplicably cold. Angus fitted the key in the lock and turned it. He pushed the door open and for a moment we could see nothing; then Angus found the light switch and stepped inside. I followed him without speaking. There were cobwebs everywhere, a broken armchair and boxes.

"It's just a store room," I said. "Nothing to worry about."

But already Angus was bending over a box. "Mind the floor," he said. "There's a hole over there."

There were rafters, an old fireplace and small windows which looked towards the hills.

"Let's go," I suggested, shivering. "We shouldn't be here anyway."

"I could do with a penknife," replied Angus. "Or an old razor-blade." His dark hair was standing on end. He was completely absorbed in opening one of the boxes. I found a nail on the floor and gave it to him.

"What's the use of that, you idiot?" he snapped. "A screwdriver would be better."

And then I saw just that lying beside one of the boxes. I gave it to Angus and watched him lever one of the boxes open. Even then I didn't visualise how dangerous our mission was.

I saw Angus's shoulders give a twitch of excitement. He straightened his back and held up something which glinted faintly beneath the light. "Ammunition," he said.

"Ammunition," I repeated stupidly.

"There's a door down to the yard, and steps. See if it's locked," said Angus. "It's through the next room, and be careful of the floor."

"Ammunition isn't any good without guns," I said, getting out of the armchair. There were several floor-boards missing and a pile of long shaped boxes in the next room. I found the door and tried the handle. It was locked.

When I returned to the other room Fiona was standing in the doorway. Her long hair hung to her shoulders. Her face was completely white. She was trembling, while her eyes took everything in. Angus had finished putting the lid back on the box. He straightened up and smiled. "You must be a light sleeper," he said. "Do come in."

"You're fools," she said slowly. "Why couldn't you leave things as they were? Why did you come here?"

I looked at Angus. "Because I suspected something," he answered. "Who does this belong to, by the way? It's a pretty dangerous lot I should think in certain hands."

"Mother doesn't know, truly she doesn't," replied Fiona. "She wouldn't understand. It all belongs to my father. He is in the gun business."

"Gun-running, you mean," exclaimed Angus.

"Now please come out," said Fiona. She spoke with great pathos. I had the feeling that we were beginning to meet the real Fiona at last.

"You must mention this to no one," she said, locking the door. "Mother must never know."

I could think of nothing to say. I knew nothing of gun-running.

"You must not speak," continued Fiona in a dramatic voice. "You will stay silent." And I thought, she doesn't know Angus!

He said, "Yes, Mam," but there was laughter behind the words which Fiona, in her distraught state, wholly missed.

"I trust you," she said. "If you say anything it will hurt my mother too, truly it will."

"Is it for shooting rabbits?" I asked.

"Of course," she agreed quickly. "And you will say nothing." I nodded slowly, longing suddenly for the warmth and safety of bed.

"Good-night . . ."

We parted in the passage, my mind in a whirl. I wished that we had never ventured into the attic. I cursed myself for failing to stop Angus. I thought of all the things I might have done—I could have snatched the key and thrown it into the weeds below my window. I could have threatened to waken Cousin Mary if he had put so much as a foot on the stairs to the attic. Instead I had gone with him and so became guilty too. There will be scandal, I thought, kicking off my trainers and climbing into bed. We will be turned out and have nowhere to go. And I saw the three of us, Angus, Phantom and myself living rough among the hills. I could not sleep. Gradually the first signs of dawn came—streaks of light on the dark cloth of the sky. And as the streaks grew wider and the cocks began to crow I imagined us camping amidst the gorse, catching fish in the deserted lake, living a Robinson Crusoe existence which suddenly seemed quite pleasant. Then at last, I slept.

6

Rain was pattering on my window when I woke up again. I could hear children talking in the distance on their way to school. I dressed quickly and ran dowstairs. Breakfast awaited me in an empty dining-room. There was a note propped up against my plate which read: *Gone fishing. Angus.* What for, I wondered? There was a letter from Dad, newly-made toast and a pot of tea with a tea-cosy over it. Obviously everyone else had eaten and departed. I wasn't sorry since I had no wish to meet Fiona this morning. I buttered my toast and opened my letter. It was short. He hoped that we were behaving ourselves, helping Cousin Mary and being friends with Fiona. Mum had been ill, but was much better now. They might be home in a week as negotiations were moving fast. He sent love and wondered why I hadn't written. I felt guilty when I put down the letter, for we had hardly helped Cousin Mary at all and Fiona was no doubt hating me this morning. The rain had stopped, so after I had washed up my plate and knife I hurried down to the stable to see Phantom. On the way I caught a glimpse of Fiona picking gooseberries behind a wall. I will write to Dad tonight and tell him about the ammunition, I decided. He will know exactly what we should do.

Phantom winnied when he heard my footsteps on the roughly-paved yard. Phantom had been fed and watered

49

and his stall had been mucked out. There was no sign of Donnie O'Reagan, but Mrs O'Reagan opened a window to call, "He's gone to a sale. He'll be back by dinner-time."

I groomed Phantom until his mane and tail were like spun silk and put some oil on his hoofs. He was impatient to be out. He stepped on my feet and banged me with his head; he opened his mouth for the bit the moment I put the reins over his head. And all the time, I was trying to forget the night, hoping in the back of my mind that Angus might see sense and keep his mouth shut. It's none of our business, I thought for the twentieth time. It's nothing to do with us.

I led Phantom out, mounted and rode into one of the small fields where I marked out a school with boulders. I trotted round and round, circling, changing the rein, doing shoulder in. I cantered. I halted. I reined back, and all the time I was seeing Fiona standing in the doorway in her white nightie saying, "Why couldn't you leave things as they were?" Then I observed Cousin Mary watching me over the gate.

"He's very beautiful," she called. "Did you have a good breakfast? Did Fiona look after you all right? I had to go shopping."

"Yes, thank you," I answered, though, of course, Fiona had not looked after me. "Isn't it a fabulous day?"

"We'll go somewhere this afternoon after an early lunch. We'll go to Pearse's cottage, so don't be long," she called.

The sun was really up now. It shone warm on my back. I jumped Phantom over a wall, then another and another until we were on the hills riding towards the gorse on the top. Sheep watched us from behind boulders. Ammunition, I thought. Why should anyone want it here?

The ground was wet underfoot. Phantom picked his way carefully. He shied at an old shoe lying in a bog. He danced sideways. He threw his head about and I knew he wanted a wide open space, a chance to stretch himself.

Presently I turned homewards. Angus was waiting for me in the yard. "Hurry up," he called. "Lunch is waiting."

"I ought to clean my tack," I replied dismounting.

"You can't. We're going out. It's going to take hours to get there and hours to get back."

"We are going to Pearse's cottage," I replied.

"How did you know?"

"Cousin Mary told me. Who was he?"

"He fought the British."

"Oh no," I exclaimed. "Did we kill him?"

"I expect so . . ."

Angus helped me untack Phantom. "How was the fishing?" I asked.

"Nothing much. I went with some local boys, but they had to go to school after a bit. Apparently Fiona's father and grandfather both grew up here."

"Where is her father?"

"In the United States."

"Does he ever come back?"

"I don't think so."

We were walking towards the house now. Lunch was on the table. Fiona was wearing a striped summer dress and sat staring out of the window.

"Did you have a good ride? I saw you on the hills," said Cousin Mary. "There are a lot of bogs up there, so be careful."

"I will," I promised. "I try to stick to the paths."

"And don't go too far; if a fog comes down you can't see a thing. People have perished there," continued Cousin Mary.

51

Lunch was soon over. Because Angus insisted on it I changed into a dress and he put on clean jeans and a striped shirt. Cousin Mary brought the car round to the front door. The dogs watched us leave with disappointed faces. Their names were Connelly, Connie for short, and Sean. England seemed far away.

It was a long drive. When we reached the cottage we found it staring at the hills. The doors were locked and there was no one to show us round. We seemed to have come a long way for very little, but it was very peaceful. Nothing seemed to move.

There were wild donkeys on the hills and turf cutters were drinking tea out of Thermoses. Fiona hardly spoke on the trip home and when she did she looked out of the window. I could think of nothing to say, but Angus made jokes, telling Cousin Mary about his exams and about Mr Bone whom everyone called Skeleton, and then about Aunt Nina's hats. Cousin Mary laughed and said that she would miss us no end when we had gone. When we reached home there were some bits of cardboard blowing about the yard and tyre marks on the gravel, but no one seemed to notice or, if they did, they made no comment. Donnie O'Reagan was lunging a magnificent grey in the paddock behind his house. Angus and I wandered round to the stables and having said good-night to Phantom we watched Donnie and the grey. "He's fabulous isn't he? I wouldn't grow out of him, not in a hundred years. But I bet he's a packet," Angus exclaimed.

The horse had the sort of head that pulls at your heart-strings, his eye was large, his cheek broad, his nose tapering. His neck was a little short of muscle, but that would come. He had plenty of heart room, a long sloping shoulder, a well set on tail and magnificent quarters. His hoofs were round, his pasterns sloping. He had a long low stride and he went quietly and confidently like someone who knows where he's going. Angus's eyes had gone all glassy. He had fallen for the horse completely. I knew the feeling. I had felt the same over Phantom.

"How much?" he called. "How much do you want for him, Donnie?" There were anxiety and excitement in his voice fairly mixed.

"I wouldn't be knowing. Four thousand, five . . ." Donnie O'Reagan waved his arm upwards as though the sky was the limit and I saw the hope disappear from Angus's face. "I shall never get a horse," he muttered. "I know I shan't." And I couldn't think of anything to say.

"He may go to America," called Donnie O'Reagan. "There's a man coming over next month. He always visits me. He's a real horseman, you understand."

I understood. The grey would do well in Virginia where they like big horses.

We went slowly towards the house. "Tomorrow we move into action," said my brother. "We will have the whole day to ourselves."

"But what can we do?" I asked. "Why can't we just let things drift? The ammunition isn't harming anyone."

My brother stared at me as though I were mad. "Haven't you ever heard of gun-running?" he asked. "Don't you realise what harm all these guns and ammunition could do?"

"Of course. But they are not harming anyone at the moment are they?" I argued.

"They could kill hundreds of innocent people, start a revolution—even a war. We can't just leave them there," cried Angus. "Have you no conscience?"

"Don't do anything until I've written to Dad for advice," I said, as we entered the house.

"That will take days," cried Angus. "We can't wait. We must act before anything awful happens . . ."

I knew I couldn't change his mind. He was too impatient to wait. For him everything must be cut and dried.

"I shall think about it all night," he continued as though he were making a concession. "And tomorrow I shall know what to do."

Fiona opened the kitchen door to call "Supper-time."

"She's been listening," I muttered.

"She can't have heard. The door was shut and we weren't talking loudly," replied Angus in a hushed voice.

"But our voices are loud, everyone says so." I was afraid now. "Please don't do anything yet," I pleaded. "Let's tell Cousin Mary what we've discovered."

We were passing through the dining-room towards the kitchen and we both automatically fell silent. I looked around me and again I had the feeling that time was running out. I wished that I could control Angus somehow. I wanted to make him look before he leapt into goodness knows what disaster.

After supper and the washing-up I knocked on his bedroom door and went inside.

"Don't do anything until you've spoken to Cousin Mary," I implored him. "Don't tell the police. She might go to prison."

"The ammunition is there to kill someone," replied Angus. "And it isn't army ammunition, because this isn't an army dump. Anyway, I don't know what I'm going to do yet. Most likely I shall visit the attic again tomorrow; so don't panic."

I returned to my room and wrote a long letter to Mum and Dad, telling them everything. I covered four foolscap pages on both sides and put Cousin Mary's telephone number at the bottom. It was the longest letter I have ever written. I put it in an envelope and wrote AIRMAIL in one corner. Afterwards, I felt much better.

It was nearly midnight by the time I had finished. I thought, *Tomorrow and tomorrow and tomorrow, creeps in this petty pace from day to day, until the last moment of recorded time*, for we had been doing Macbeth at school.

I thought of the grey and how he would suit Angus if we ever had enough money to buy him. I thought of Phantom's outstanding beauty, and how he was really too beautiful for the rough hills outside and more suited to a film set in California. Sleep wouldn't come. Gradually I started to fear everything, the shadows in the room, Fiona. I imagined Dad kidnapped, gagged and tied to a chair, Mum dying of cholera, Angus riding into an ambush, and then, without warning I fell asleep as the roosters started to proclaim a new day.

7

I wakened to find Fiona standing beside my bed. She was dressed for Dublin, in cotton dress, white sandals and a cardigan. "We are going now," she said. "Breakfast is on the table. Mrs O'Flatery will wash it up and make the beds. She is a very competent woman." I rubbed the sleep from my eyes. Fiona was not looking at me. "And I should leave well alone, truly I would," she added, staring through the window at the sky outside.

"Thank you. I'm sorry I overslept."

She shut the door behind her and presently I heard the sound of a car going away down the drive. Angus met me in the passage. "They've gone," he said unnecessarily. "We've got the whole day to ourselves."

"Why don't we go for a picnic? You can have Peppermint. We can ride right over the hills, and it would do Phantom good; he's not getting enough exercise."

"I will think about it," replied Angus. "The attic key has disappeared from under the stairs. I suppose Fiona has hidden it somewhere. Now why should a prospective nun be mixed up with gun-running?"

"Let's enjoy ourselves, just for today," I pleaded.

But I have never been able to influence Angus and today was no exception. He hurried into breakfast whistling in an infuriating way which made me want to throw the salt-cellar at him. "Fantastic, scrambled eggs.

56

They're a bit watery on top and lukewarm, but otherwise smashing," he cried, taking three-quarters for himself.

"You're the most selfish person I ever met," I answered. "Look at your helping."

"Boys need more than girls."

"That's what you think."

Suddenly I hated him. "You spoil everything," I shouted. "You just want Cousin Mary to go to prison. As long as you get your way you don't care what happens to anyone else."

"Oh shut up, pieface," replied Angus, helping himself to toast. "You're yellow, that's your trouble."

"I'm not, and you know it," I shouted. "Who got you down that mountain in Virginia when you were lying unconscious?"

"That wasn't anything. Anyway, the men carried me down," replied Angus, pouring himself two cupfuls of milk one after another. "It's all right, I've left some for you," he added. "And now I'm going out for a ride. I'm going to look for some geology specimens and do some thinking. And I don't want you; you're much too cross."

"Thank you very much. I wouldn't go with you if you went down on your knees and begged me," I cried. "And you've only left me a thimbleful of milk. Look!"

"That's your hard luck," replied Angus, leaving the table. "First come, first served, that's my motto."

"I've written to Mum and Dad. I've told them everything, so they will know whom to blame if things go wrong."

"Thank you, that's very noble of you," replied Angus sarcastically.

"You're supposed to take your dirty crocks to the kitchen," I added as he strode out of the room, his hands deep in his pockets, looking suddenly like a younger version of Dad. "I'm not taking them."

"They can stay then," shouted Angus, laughing.

I cleared the table and was still hating him when I went upstairs to fetch my letter, but it wasn't there. I stared at the table where I had put it. Then I went through all my pockets; after that I looked on the hall table and all over the dining-room. It was not addressed, so no one would have posted it—either Fiona or Angus had taken it, but which?

Mrs O'Flatery had arrived by this time. She wore an old cotton frock and there were varicose veins on her legs like grapes, as a result of having seven children. She put an arm round me and asked how I was liking Ireland, and said that England was a terrible place these days, with all creeds and cults fighting each other and murders every hour. We chatted for a bit and then I went down the drive to the stables where I found Donnie O'Reagan grooming Phantom.

"Let me," I said, "honestly."

"Your brother has been gone thirty minutes or more," he said in his soft Irish voice. "He will be waiting for you no doubt."

"I'm not going with him," I replied. "He wants to be alone."

Donnie O'Reagan shook his head and handed me the brush he was using. "The Pony Club meets over the hill next week," he told me. "You can go if you like."

"That's a super idea," I answered. "Do they mind visitors?"

"You would be welcome, I'm sure of that."

I groomed Phantom for ages; there seemed nothing else to do. When I led him out of the stable at last there was a light drizzle falling which hid the hills from view. I schooled Phantom in spite of the rain. Slowly a mist descended and I thought, Angus will be back soon and

I shan't speak to him, not a word. I hacked Phantom up the road and back, and when I put him away Angus still hadn't come home. Mrs O'Flatery was just leaving when I went inside. "I've put your dinner ready for you," she said. "It's only something cold."

"Thank you very much."

"You're welcome. You will be all right now, won't you?" she asked.

"Of course."

The house felt empty when she had gone. I stood at the window staring at the falling rain. It's just like Angus to be late, I thought. If I was selfish I would begin lunch. I would eat all the best bits. But two wrongs don't make a right, so I'll wait. I found a newspaper and started to read, but I couldn't concentrate. I stood up and looked out. The hills were blanketed in rain, and where was Angus? The first pangs of anxiety started to gnaw. He can't still be gathering stones, I thought, not in the rain. He's not that keen. The dogs watched my face; they were lonely too. I started to walk about the house and they followed me from room to room with dismal faces. It's just a terrible day, I thought, first there was breakfast, then my letter disappearing and now this. I would have given anything to hear Angus coming in. I looked at lunch; there were a few over-cooked potatoes, ham salad, and stewed gooseberries; but I wasn't hungry. I looked out of the window again and the landscape seemed to mock me. The clock in the hall said twenty to two ... and now my knees started to feel weak and I could hear my heart thumping against my ribs. I will eat something to give me strength, I thought, and then I will saddle Phantom and go out and look for him. I won't get lost because Phantom will know the way back. I forced myself to eat some ham and salad. The rain was coming down in torrents.

I shut my eyes and prayed, "Please God let him be

59

coming along the drive now. Let him be all right."
I opened them, expecting a miracle, but the drive was
still empty. I fetched my riding mackintosh from
upstairs and the dogs followed. Never had the house
seemed so gloomy, so remote and forgotten. "You can't
come," I told the dogs. "Can't you see it's raining?
Cousin Mary and Fiona will be back soon, God
willing." I heard footsteps on the drive and rushed to
the front door, but it was only one of the O'Reagan
children with a mackintosh over his head.

"The horse is back," he shouted.

"What?" I cried stupidly. "What horse?"

"Your brother's horse. He's come back on his own.
He's in the stable."

I slammed the front door and ran towards the stable.
My heart was like a sledge-hammer banging against my
ribs. "I knew something awful had happened," I cried.
"What shall I do?"

But the child did not know. He said, "Father's not at
home, Mother sent me."

"I will go up on the hills on my horse," I answered.

"They are awful wild."

"I know."

Mrs O'Reagan was holding Peppermint. "I don't
know how to take his tackle off," she said.

She was soaking wet. "The little one is ill," she said.
"I can't stay. He's awfully bad. We will be seeing Dr
O'Sullivan any minute now. He will make him better,
God willing."

I took hold of Peppermint. His reins were broken and
one stirrup and leather were missing. "He needs a rub
down," I said, but Mrs O'Reagan had left already with
the boy to wait the arrival of Dr O'Sullivan. I felt
terribly alone now. I took off Peppermint's tack and
rubbed him as quickly as I could with a cloth. Then I
fetched Phantom's tack from the saddle room. All the

time I was trying not to think too hard, trying not to let my imagination work, trying not to panic, and the rain kept falling bucketful after bucketful onto the wild brown hills.

Phantom opened his mouth and took the bit. I knew he would go in spite of the rain, go till he dropped. I led him out, mounted and turned his head to the hills. Now that I was in the saddle, hope started to come back. He may be sheltering behind a rock, I thought, or have reached a road and be walking home.

The priest had arrived on a bicycle. He went into the O'Reagans' cottage, soon to be followed by a doctor carrying a case. I wish Cousin Mary was at home, I thought. I wish we had gone to Dublin with them. Nothing can be worse than this. The rain smacked against my face. There was nothing to be seen on the hills. They seemed to go on and on for ever, to be as endless as a rain-soaked sea. Phantom's hoofs squelched in the peaty earth. It was difficult to ride fast. Every few minutes I stopped to call, "Angus, where are you? Angus . . ." And nothing answered, nothing at all.

Grease ran off the reins onto my hands. I couldn't see the summits of the hills. It was like riding half blindfolded. Most of the time my head was bent against the rain. And I thought, supposing I don't find him, not ever? What shall I do then? I remembered that Dad had given Angus a number in London to ring, but only in case of acute emergency, he had said. But surely this was just such an occasion? I stopped again to call "Angus", but my voice was drowned by the falling rain. I started to hate Ireland. In England there would be a road nearby. I could stop and ask motorists to look for him; I could find people to help. I felt utterly alone. We had reached the summit of the first hill, but there was nothing to be seen beyond but another valley swept by more sheets of rain. Perhaps I should go back and telephone that number, I thought, longing for comforting advice, for someone to say, "Don't worry, I'll take over. Everything will be all right." But where was the number? It could be in Angus's pocket at this very moment, or hidden somewhere in his room. He could have lost it, learnt it by memory, done anything with it . . . "Angus," I shouted into the rain, "Angus, where are you?"

I had hated him at breakfast and now he might be dying somewhere with a cracked skull or wandering concussed in the rain. If I had gone with him, everything would have been all right. I could have led him home on Peppermint. I had forgotten to put on my watch, but I reckoned the time must be three o'clock, and he had left soon after nine in the morning; that made seven hours. Seven hours wandering on the hills! I should have started looking hours ago. And why had Peppermint taken so long coming home? I hated myself now. I've let everyone down, I thought. How shall I explain my behaviour to our parents? How shall I explain waiting five hours before beginning to search?

At last the rain lightened. I could see the valley below more clearly now, with a track winding through it and great clumps of gorse and a little herd of donkeys with their backs to the rain.

"Angus," I shouted. "Angus . . ."

There were bogs on each side of us and sudden cliffs where turf had been cut. I pushed Phantom into a trot. Phantom tossed his head and neighed but nothing answered. "Angus," I shouted again, "Angus." My voice echoed and my cries returned to mock me.

I don't know how far I rode. At one stage I felt salt on my face and realised I was crying. Phantom did not tire but I could sense time passing, afternoon turning to evening, milking time coming and going. At home in England horses would be coming out from under trees

62

to graze in the cool of the evening. Our cottage would wear the dreamy look of dusk. At this time Dad would normally be returning from London, entering the hall in town clothes. I looked at the hills, hating them, and tried to make up my mind whether to go on or turn back. And all the time I could feel panic growing inside me and a terrifying feeling of dread.

I could see a lake below me as empty as the landscape, with dark woods behind. I turned homewards and thought how foolish I would seem if I found Angus waiting for me in the house. I imagined him running out, calling, "Where *have* you been? I got back hours ago."

I pushed Phantom into a canter. "We're going home," I said, "and if Angus isn't there, we'll telephone the police." And I felt better, simply because at last I had decided something.

8

But no one greeted me. The house was still deserted. The curtains were drawn in the front of the O'Reagans' cottage, the priest's bike propped outside. I was afraid that the sick child was dying. I didn't want to trouble them although I was in such dire straits myself. Peppermint was shivering in the stable. He looked well on his way to pneumonia, which made me feel hideously guilty for everything. I had ridden Phantom so fast that his sides were still going in and out like bellows. I fetched hay and rubbed him and Peppermint down, though I knew that really I should be indoors ringing the police. And still Fiona and Cousin Mary had not come home. The dogs greeted me when I went indoors. They looked anxious too, and their ears were perpetually pricked listening for Cousin Mary's familiar footstep. "Good doggies," I said. "She'll be back soon, I promise."

The telephone was in the sitting-room. I picked it up and waited. No one answered. I tried again. I fetched my watch and timed myself until I had waited for ten minutes and still there was no answer. It was obvious to me then that it had been cut off. I started to feel sick suddenly, for now the whole of Ireland seemed against me—everyone. I imagined enemies in every room. I was afraid to go outside and yet I had to do something. It was then that I saw the envelope lying on the hall mat. I picked it up and read, *To the English girl. Open at once* and my heart started to race again. I couldn't stop my hand shaking. I opened the envelope and read:

If you want your brother to stay alive come to the tower at six o'clock and bring £500. If you tell anyone we will know how to deal with your brother and yourself for that matter. Come at once if you value your brother's life.

It wasn't signed. At first I felt nothing but an overwhelming sense of relief, for at least Angus was still alive. Then I looked at my watch and saw that it was past seven, which meant I was an hour late already and it was miles to the tower. And which tower anyway? And how was I to get there? Then without thinking I was running towards the stable, throwing a saddle on Phantom's back; but now I remembered the money, so I raced back to the house and found the ten pounds we had left among Angus's socks in the drawer. Five hundred pounds! They must be mad, I thought. How can we possibly have that much money with us? And then I thought how odd it was Angus being kidnapped instead of Dad—if only I could laugh. Phantom looked dejected as I led him out of the stable once more. The sun had set. The nearest tower stood in the opposite direction to the path I had taken earlier. There was no path that way. It was going to be a hard ride and Phantom was tired already.

He left the yard reluctantly, looking back to neigh to the other horses. I carried the kidnap note and the money in my jodphurs' pocket. The dogs watched me leave from one of the windows of the house. An ambulance drew up outside the O'Reagans' cottage. Fear evaporated as I rode. Riding Phantom, I felt ready to face anything.

But the tower did not seem to grow any nearer.

Phantom stumbled over the uneven ground. Several times I dismounted to lead him, all the while I was aware of the approaching night which would soon darken the distant hills. I pushed Phantom on with my legs. It was seven-thirty now and I seemed to have ten miles or more still between me and the tower. I imagined Angus tied up. What was he thinking? Did he know about the note? Would he be pleased when he saw me? I hit Phantom with the reins. Mercy and kindness deserted me. I imagined Angus led out and shot because I was late. I imagined telling my parents . . . life without Angus . . . life going on just the same. Phantom started to gallop, avoiding the boulders by a miracle, stretching his beautiful neck, struggling, sweating through peaty earth, going on and on with all the courage he had towards the tower.

Twice he all but fell; once I found myself on his neck, my legs wrapped round his withers. But we were nearly there now; darkness had not come, the dying day still hovered between dusk and night. I drew rein and let him walk and thought, supposing the tower's empty, what then? And now my heart was thudding against my ribs again and all my courage seemed gone. I drew rein and called, "Anyone about? I've come for my brother."

And from somewhere quite near a donkey brayed.

A boy came out from the tower, carrying a gun as carelessly as one carries a shopping bag.

"So you've come, and where would the money be?" he asked, holding out a hand. "It isn't much we are asking," he continued, looking me straight in the eye. "And maybe you can have some of it back later if you behave yourselves." He had a lilt to his voice. He seemed to belong to the dark hills and the rain.

"I want to see my brother first. Where is he?" I demanded trying not to sound frightened, though now,

66

without warning, my teeth had started to chatter. I rode resolutely towards the tower.

"He isn't there," replied the boy. "My friends are guarding him. I will let you have him when I have the money."

"But we haven't five hundred pounds," I replied, controlling my chattering teeth with difficulty. "We are on holiday."

"You should have asked someone then." His mouth was a thin determined line. I was afraid of him now. He played with his gun and looked at me sideways.

"You must be mad," I said.

"You can't have your brother then," he replied turning away. "We need the money; and we need your mouths shut."

"Please be sensible," I pleaded. "Take what I have, and I swear we'll keep our mouths shut. It will be dark soon and we'll die on these hills, and Cousin Mary will send the police after you, and then you'll be in trouble."

The pound notes were sodden with rain when I took them from my pocket, but he was laughing now. "We don't care about trouble, we're always in trouble. We live on trouble, you understand," he said. "And I'm willing enough to shoot a rich man any time; they are all vermin in my eyes."

I felt very cold, too cold to speak.

"It is easy enough," he continued. "If you have so little money, I will take your horse. He is a beautiful animal, but you must keep your mouth shut about what you have seen in the attic, or we will kill him you understand. But if you keep quiet, I may let you have him back some time, you understand." I wanted to scream at him, but no words came. My legs were like jelly. Inside I was frozen. I looked at Phantom's beautiful head, now soaked in sweat and rain; his eyes still full of courage; his heart still ready to go on till he

67

dropped. And I could find no words for the misery and horror I was feeling.

"I can shoot anything," said the boy with a laugh in his voice, pointing his gun at Phantom's head. "I never miss. Now give him to me before I get angry."

"No. I will go back and cable London for money."

The boy whistled and two men came over the hill. One of them said, "We've put the gelignite under the hut. We can blow it all up, the boy too, at a moment's notice. It only needs a match."

They stood staring at Phantom. They were true Irishmen, for they couldn't stop looking. "He is a winner, truly he is," one said in admiration.

I was crying without knowing. I knew already what I had to do. You can't really match a horse against a person, not when it's your own brother. I had to say, "Take him," but the words wouldn't come; they stuck in my throat while I remembered the past—bringing Phantom down sick from the Blue Ridge Mountains, nursing him back to health, bringing him back to England. It had always seemed like a dream—too good to be true, too wonderful to last. And now the end had come on a brown peaty hillside in a remote part of Ireland with the darkness coming down and nothing there but the sheep and us, and all because Angus had had to look in Cousin Mary's attic. It had started like a dream, and now it was ending in an equally crazy way. I looked at the boy and the two men and I thought, if only this could be a nightmare, if only I could wake up at home and know it had never really happened; that we were all still in England, that Phantom was outside grazing under the elms. I dismounted. "Do you want the tack as well?" It wasn't me who spoke. It was like someone else speaking a long way off.

He nodded and vaulted on. He wrenched Phantom's

head round and cantered away beyond the tower. My tears ran down onto the damp earth.

"We will take you to him. But I advise you not to mention what you found in the attic, if only for your little cousin's sake."

I followed them without speaking. I felt numb, like a beaten animal. They took me to a turf cutter's hut with a corrugated iron roof. They unlocked a heavy padlock and one of them said, "There you are, miss. You'll find your brother somewhere in there."

I wanted to shout, "I hate you," but the words wouldn't come. I could only see Phantom going away into the dusk, going away and never coming back. The hut was dark inside. I untied Angus's hands and he said, "I thought you were never coming. Am I glad to see you. How much did you pay? I hope you didn't give them anything? You didn't did you? And did you ring the London number?" His hands were all red and he was covered with mud. His face looked pale and immature after the Irishmen's faces.

"I paid them everything," I said. "I paid them Phantom."

He didn't understand at first. "What do you mean? Explain. Hurry up."

"I traded him for you," I answered. "And there's nothing more to say, nothing at all."

There was a silence while Angus took in my words. Then he said, "We'll get him back, I promise you." And we left the hut with the door open.

"They said they might send him back if we didn't mention what was in the attic, but if we do they will kill him," I said, following Angus, and I imagined Phantom lying dead. "It's so funny," I continued. "We were afraid Mum and Dad would be kidnapped and it was you in the end—you were kidnapped." And I started to laugh in a mad way which was half crying

69

until Angus said, "Shut up, let me think, and where are we going, for pity's sake? We should have found a road. We'll be completely lost in a minute."

"I don't mind if we are, I don't mind dying," I cried. "I don't want to go on living without Phantom, don't you understand?"

"You should never have traded him then, you should have called their bluff," replied my brother.

"There wasn't any bluff. They were going to shoot you or blow up the hut. They are mad, quite mad. Can't you understand?" I wanted to add, "Do you think I wanted to trade Phantom for you—you who are always so selfish?" But I couldn't because it wasn't true. Angus was as much part of my life as Phantom, and we had shared more together.

"It's nearly dark," said Angus. "We had better run; if we get to the top of that hill we will probably see lights below."

But my legs would not run any more. My knees ached, I felt limp all over and I was still seeing Phantom disappearing out of my life for ever—in the circumstances I did not mind what happened to me, not any more.

"You are not trying," shouted Angus. "Run."

"I can't," I shouted back into the gathering darkness. "I'm finished—spent. I've got nothing left. You ate all the breakfast—remember? And I was too worried to eat much lunch." There was a humming noise in my ears and my head ached unbearably. I sat down on a boulder. For a moment everything went black. "It's all right, I must have fainted," I called, but Angus was now far ahead shouting, "Come on, do come on. It will be pitch black in a minute. We won't see anything. Cousin Mary will send out a search-party."

I thought of policemen coming, tall strong men who would carry me gently home to my bed where I could lie and sleep and forget, if even for a few hours, that I had lost Phantom. I wondered where he was now, where the boy was going with him. Would he be hidden away somewhere? Angus was beside me now, shaking me. "Move," he shouted. "Please move."

"I am," I said telling my legs to move, standing up. "I'm trying." I felt drunk with exhaustion but I walked on, up and up towards the summit, putting one leg in front of the other in dreary repetition, stumbling over boulders, banging my knees, while darkness came. I shouted, "I'm only doing this for you, Angus, not for myself, because personally I don't want to go on living, not without Phantom, not any more."

He shouted back, "We'll find Phantom, I promise."

I struggled on, praying for a moon. Peaty water oozed over the top of my jodphur boots. A rabbit vanished in front of me, its white tail bobbing. Three or four sheep got up hurriedly at my approach and scuttled away baaing into the darkness. Far away a car hooted its horn. We couldn't see the tower any more. We had reached the top of the hill, but there were no lights on the other side, just more wiry grass, boulders, soggy earth and the dark empty sky overhead. My legs moved mechanically, my mind wandered. I imagined the future without Phantom. What would I do? How would I spend my weekends? I had no close friends. We had moved about so often in our lives that my local friends had disappeared, or made other friends; so I had been alone in that sense for some time, but it had not mattered because I had had Phantom.

I tried to run down the hill to another valley and another hill on the other side, but suddenly I seemed to be falling into space; then I hit dark earth with my right foot buckled under me against a boulder. I saw stars and then my foot started to hurt. I shouted, "Wait, Angus, Angus."

And it seemed ages before he came back and cried, "Oh no, you didn't fall into the turf cuttings! How could you?"

"It's my foot," I answered, trying to stand. "I think I've done something to it." I felt it through my jodphur boot and I wanted to scream with pain.

"Lie back," Angus said. "I'll go on and bring back help."

"Supposing those men find me?" I asked plaintively.

"They won't, they've gone," replied Angus setting off down the hill, whistling to keep his spirits up. "I'll bring a Land Rover, don't worry," he called back over his shoulder and, for a second, I could hear his hurrying feet. Then I was completely alone and the only sound was that of running water. I leaned my head back against some peat and tried to move my foot, but it hurt too much. The sky was full of stars now and at last the moon had risen, a small faint new moon which cast only a shadowy light on the desolate moors. I tried to stay awake; but the day seemed to have lasted for ever so that breakfast seemed like last week, lunch like yesterday. It seemed impossible that so much could happen in one day. I then started to think about Phantom and tears cascaded down my cheeks in an unstoppable flood.

9

Suddenly I was wakened by lights. I tried to sit up, but I was stiff all through and the water under the peaty earth had soaked through my clothes. I had been dreaming of home. It was a terrible shock to come back to reality, to know that Phantom had gone, that the pain in my foot was hardly bearable and that somehow I had to keep secret the truth of what had happened. I could hear Donnie O'Reagan's voice now and it was as soft as the sound of the water dripping through the peat.

He had another man with him and they had brought a horse rug. It was large and smelt deliciously of horse. He talked to me in the soothing voice he used with his horses, which would calm the most excitable four-year-old. "Just ease her in . . . she's in awful pain. Gently now. We won't hurt you . . . It's all right, my darling . . . steady now."

They slid the rug under my aching body. I did not want to talk nor think, but just to exist for the time being, until somehow things came right again.

They carried me gently, talking quietly to one another and I learned that the sick O'Reagan was in hospital with peritonitis, and that all afternoon he had been between life and death. The moon looked larger now and the moors were like fairyland. And at last we could see the lights below, the lights which led us home.

I started to wonder what Cousin Mary would have to say and how Angus had fared. The grey house looked desolate and lost in the moonlight, and I wished that I could be taken to Donnie O'Reagan's overcrowded cottage instead.

"You're awful light," said Donnie O'Reagan as he reached the gate which led us across a paddock to the house. "You must be eating more and don't worry about your little horse, my darling, we will be finding him in the morning for sure."

Cousin Mary opened the front door. She looked desperately tired and her wispy hair had come unpinned.

"You found her then, O'Reagan, good man," she said. I wished that she would call him Donnie, or Mr O'Reagan. Just O'Reagan seemed so remote for such a kind man.

"We will take her upstairs, she will be needing the doctor for sure," said Donnie O'Reagan. "Her foot looks awful bad. And she lost her little horse and it's breaking her heart."

I wondered how he knew. "It's an awful shock to lose a horse," he continued, "a terrible shock for a young girl."

They slid me on to the bed still in my wet clothes. Angus was standing in the doorway, barefooted, with his hair on end and his pyjamas parting body and soul as usual. He glanced anxiously at me. "You look awful," he said. "I think you should be in hospital."

Cousin Mary tried to give Donnie O'Reagan and his helper some money, but they shook their heads muttering, "We couldn't, thank you Madam, not for the poor soul. You're welcome."

I wished they could stay, for at that moment they seemed the kindest people in the world. But their boots clumped steadily down the stairs and Cousin Mary said,

"Let's get your clothes off you. It's nearly midnight and they're soaked through."

Angus fetched me three hot-water bottles, two aspirins and a glass of water in the meantime. I heard Cousin Mary mutter, "No food tonight," and something about hospital and an anaesthetic in the morning. She put me in the frilly nightie Aunt Nina had given me, so it was some use after all. She gave me the aspirins and held the glass of water to my lips while Angus opened the bottom of my bed and slid the hot water-bottles inside.

"You should be in bed, Angus. You caused all the trouble," Cousin Mary said. "Boys! Thank God I never had a boy. Why did you go out alone? And did you have to fall off? What your parents will say I can't think. I shall never trust you again. Now go to bed."

I was sorry for Angus, but could think of nothing to say except, "It wasn't his fault there are mad men on the hills." But, of course, I couldn't say that.

Cousin Mary fetched some water in a bowl, soap, my sponge and a towel. I said, "It's all right, I can wash myself. I'm all right, or I will be in the morning. It's just my foot." And now in the distance the cocks were crowing. It was another day already, my first day without Phantom.

"We had a puncture," said Cousin Mary, "and I couldn't undo the nuts. Otherwise we would have been back by six o'clock. Now go to sleep and don't worry about Phantom. He will turn up for sure."

When I wakened again a man in a suit was standing over me with a clean white handkerchief in his breast pocket. "You have been in the wars," he said. "Let's look at your foot." He was tall and fairheaded. The sun was streaming through the window. Fiona stood just behind him and Cousin Mary was on the other side of the bed. They looked like anxious hens.

"She'll have to go into hospital. I'll send for an ambulance," he announced replacing the bedclothes. "They'll give her an anaesthetic, so I should forget about anything to eat for the time being."

"Can Angus go with me?" I asked. "Please . . ."

"I don't think that will be very suitable," replied Cousin Mary. "He's caused enough trouble already."

They left together and I saw that my room had been dusted and there were fresh flowers on the table. Presently Cousin Mary returned. "You're to swallow two of these tablets," she said, "Doctor's orders. The ambulance will be here quite soon. Where's your dressing-gown?"

I wanted to hop downstairs, but the ambulance men carried me down on a stretcher. I felt idiotic being carried, and all the time I was trying not to think about Phantom. Angus was standing outside on the gravel, looking lost and unwanted. He didn't say anything; perhaps he was too depressed or was afraid that anything he said would be interpreted the wrong way.

"It wasn't his fault," I told Cousin Mary. "I didn't have to fall over the edge. He wasn't even near me."

"Exactly," replied Cousin Mary. She sat in the ambulance with me saying nothing. I couldn't look at Donnie O'Reagan's place because I was afraid it would make me cry.

"O'Reagan's looking for your horse," said Cousin Mary after a time. "He's making inquiries."

But the boy will have hidden him, I thought. He will be shut up somewhere like Angus was, banging at a door hour after hour, waiting for me. And I'll never find him. I can't even look for him when I'm like this.

"He knows everyone. It will only be a matter of time."

76

"I'm sorry we've put you to so much trouble," I said.

"It can't be helped, can it?"

"Angus didn't mean to fall off like that."

"And you didn't mean to lose your horse."

I was glad when we reached the hospital, though it was nothing but lights and nurses and an overpowering smell of disinfectant. I saw a young doctor. My foot was X-rayed and Cousin Mary followed me from department to department like an oppressed nanny. The doctors laughed and joked and the nurses were kind. Then at last someone slipped a needle into my arm and I passed out. When I came to I was on a bed with my foot in plaster. A nurse brought me a cup of tea and sandwiches. Later I hopped out to the car and we started for home. It was afternoon by this time and there seemed to be Americans everywhere, buying souvenirs. The car was like an oven because it had stood so long under the sun in the hospital car-park. Cousin Mary hardly spoke and I relapsed into dreary thoughts about Phantom. I wondered what Dad would say when we told him. He might go straight to the Irish Government or ring up the British Ambassador if there was one. And he would find out about the guns, because he always found out everything. The drive home seemed to last for ever. My foot itched inside the plaster and I felt sick because of the anaesthetic. I kept my eyes glued to the windows hoping to see Phantom standing on some distant hill; but there were only donkeys and black-faced sheep and great cone-shaped piles of turf drying in the evening sun.

Fiona and Angus had prepared a meal. There seemed an uneasy truce between them. The dogs welcomed us. I longed to call on Donnie O'Reagan, to rush into his cottage crying, "Any news?" Instead I hobbled to the kitchen sink, washed my hands and sat down to high tea. We made no conversation beyond, "Pass the butter,

77

please," or "Can I have some more?" I think we were all too tired to talk. Fiona looked as though she had not slept for a week, my brother had dark circles under his eyes, Cousin Mary seemed fraught with anxiety. Finally she said, "I wonder whether we should tell the police about your horse, Jean?" which made both Angus and me jump out of our skins.

Fiona went a little whiter and Angus asked, "Tell them what?"

"That he's lost, of course," replied Cousin Mary impatiently, "with all his tack on his back."

"Will they come here?" asked Fiona.

"Why should they? They will just know whom he belongs to if they find him wandering on the road."

She left the room to telephone. I looked at Fiona and she looked at me. How much did she know?

"I've told her what happened," my brother said. "She says they certainly won't stop at shooting Phantom if we say anything. They killed three of her pet rabbits once, didn't they, Fiona?"

She looked away, her eyes misted with tears. I couldn't speak. Again I was imagining Phantom shot, lying dead. I wished that Cousin Mary would leave the telephone, that Dad would suddenly appear and take over, that I was anywhere but here sitting at the table with poor sad Fiona, and my brother who had started everything by searching the attics.

"It's been cut off again. Off to bed with you, Jean," said Cousin Mary. "The hospital said 'rest' so rest it must be."

I went upstairs which took an age. I leaned out of my bedroom window and stared at the hills, wanting to be on them searching for Phantom, calling him, searching for hoofprints. I felt completely helpless sitting in my room. It was a lovely evening with a mist coming down on the hills and a red sky promising a fine tomorrow. Donnie O'Reagan was lunging the grey; he moved beautifully, but he had none of Phantom's spirit nor the look of wildness which went with his windswept mane. I couldn't cry any more. It was as though I had no tears left; but I felt sad to the marrow of my bones.

After a time Angus knocked on the door and came in and sat on the end of my bed. "Don't you want to know what happened to me?" he asked.

"Fire away," I answered.

"They tripped Peppermint up. They had binoculars, so they must have seen me leave the stable," he said. "It was lucky I didn't break my collarbone or something; as it was I passed out for at least three seconds and, when I came to, Peppermint was galloping away and they had my hands tied behind my back."

"How did they trip him up?"

"With wire or rope, I suppose. They called me all sorts of names and threatened to shoot me then and there. It wasn't funny I assure you. They kept on and on about the attics and I kept standing up for poor Fiona, assuring them she had not said anything. It was all pretty unnerving. They took me to the hut and gave me a cup of tea out of a Thermos. They told me how civilised they were, and in a stupid sort of way I couldn't really believe it was actually happening. I kept thinking, it must be a game, and soon they will say 'pax' and it will be over. Then they started talking about a ransom to buy more arms and what they would do to me if you didn't pay up. I wasn't really frightened, that was the funny part. I think I imagined they wouldn't dare shoot me, but now I'm not so sure because Fiona says they *have* killed one or two people."

"So they will kill Phantom," I said.

"I doubt it; he's too valuable. They may sell him

though, but we can still get him back, because you can't sell stolen property. He will still be yours."

I saw myself searching the world for Phantom, growing older, still searching. "Americans come over to buy horses, so do the Dutch. He may go anywhere. We'll never find him, I know we won't . . ."

"You're just pessimistic because of your ankle. I would go to the police, but Fiona's afraid they'll get the dogs. She's terrified of them. It's awful; no wonder she wants to be a nun."

The sun had set now. You couldn't see the hills any more. "Can't we ring the London number?" I asked. "It's probably the Foreign Office and they will know what to do for certain."

My brother looked out of the window. He seemed embarrassed. "Well," I demanded. "Why not?"

"I wish we could."

"You mean you've lost it. Oh, well done!" I cried. "Now you've really upset the apple cart; now we really are on our own. Why didn't you give it to me to look after? You always lose everything."

"Dad gave it to me because I'm the eldest. Perhaps someone took it. I left it on my chest of drawers for all the world to see."

"The person who took my letter," I added.

"You mean it never went?"

"It disappeared. I've only just remembered."

Everything suddenly seemed too big for us to manage and my foot started to ache again. "I'll write a letter now and post it in the morning. Someone must let them know what's happening," said Angus. "I dropped in on Donnie O'Reagan after tea but he hadn't had any luck. He isn't giving up hope though, he's going to a horse sale tomorrow. All his buddies will be there too."

"Did he find any signs today?"

Angus shook his head. "But he says it's only a matter

of time. He says that you can't hide a horse in Ireland for long, not one like Phantom."

"Thank you," I said.

"What for?"

"Seeing Donnie O'Reagan."

"Fiona thinks her father sends money for the guns; she isn't sure, but she thinks so," my brother said. "God, what a muddle."

"Why did we come?" I asked. "Why didn't we go to Devon?"

"Our parents didn't know it would be like this. But they will when they get my letter, wow!" exclaimed my brother, leaving the room.

I tried to sleep, but presently Fiona came in. She stared at me and asked, "Will it be hurting?" I said, "Not really. I'm sorry about your rabbits though."

"It was a real shame, they were so pretty," she answered. "Truly they were. I found them hanging from a tree in the morning. They are terrible men though, truly wicked and no one can stop them. But I am sorry for you losing your beautiful horse and all."

Suddenly I didn't want to listen. I simply wanted to lie and think about Phantom and forget the rest.

"It's all right. Do you mind if I sleep now?"

She crept from the room without a word and I climbed out of bed to look once more at the hills, but it was too dark to see anything. I sat there for ages and gradually the moon came up. I kept imagining I saw him, but when I looked closer it was only a boulder looking strange in the moonlight. I thought, they hung Fiona's rabbits from a tree, so what will they do to Phantom if we talk? And supposing Angus says too much? I can't stop him. I never can. I was filled with awful forebodings which turned to nightmares when I slept.

In spite of the nightmares I didn't want to wake up;

but morning came all too soon when Angus burst into my room talking sixteen to the dozen.

"I shall search today on Peppermint. Don't worry, I shall find him. I've posted the letter to Dad. It's gone airmail express. With luck he will telephone in a day or two and if anyone can find Phantom, he can."

I wished he would stop talking so that I could go back to sleep and forget about Phantom being gone forever.

"I want to sleep. I want to stay here all day. I don't want to get up ever again; everything's too awful. It would be different if I could put on shoes and ride, if I could look too." Suddenly I was filled with self-pity.

"But we've all had breakfast. You must get up. You're not an invalid. You've only cracked your toes."

"Only," I answered, "and lost Phantom. Besides, you're not to go out alone," I added, sitting up suddenly, completely awake. "You will only be kidnapped again and then someone else will have to pay to get you back."

"I shall be ready this time. I shall take a gun," replied Angus.

"No!" I shouted. "That's being like them. Can't you understand? Shooting people won't help. It won't bring Phantom back."

But he had left my room. I clambered out of bed and pulled on some clothes, hobbled down the stairs, out of the front door. I imagined Angus shooting and being shot, people searching the moors for him. But I found him still in Donnie O'Reagan's yard and Donnie O'Reagan was holding the gun.

He was saying, "Carrying a gun won't help you now. I have seven children or I would be out there looking for your sister's horse. But I can't risk them, you understand, please God. And you're not taking any of my horses up there, not if I can stop you."

82

"And you should be resting that foot of yours for sure," continued Donnie O'Reagan, seeing me for the first time. "That's what you should be doing."

"I want Phantom back," I said.

"We all do," replied Donnie O'Reagan.

"But nothing's being done."

"I'll find him, don't worry your poor head. I'll have him back here before the week's out." I didn't believe him. He was trying to save his own skin. I was trying to save Phantom's. There was no way out. It was like being in a tunnel with no entrance or exit. If we went to the police the boy would shoot Phantom; if we didn't we would still most likely never see him again. Did everyone know about the guns? Had they all been successfully silenced?

I hobbled back towards the house, my eyes smarting with tears. Angus followed me. "I'm going to the police," he said.

"But they won't believe your story," I answered. "And who'll support you? They're all too scared to talk."

"I shall look on a bike," said Angus. "I'm not beaten that easily."

"He could be a hundred miles away by now," I answered. "Perhaps we should tell Cousin Mary. She might understand."

"Sure," replied Angus. "She's married to a gun-runner. He sends the money for the guns no doubt, and money to keep the place going too; that's why no one liked her marrying him. It's all as plain as a pikestaff now."

I wished the sun would stop shining; that the heavens would burst, that the whole of Ireland would suddenly erupt and disappear into the sea. "It's so beautiful here," I said. "It should be happy. Even the house could be lovely."

83

I hobbled after Angus to the garage, but all our luck had run out—the one and only bike had a puncture and there was nothing to mend it with; and now Cousin Mary was calling me from the house to breakfast.

"Where have you been?" she demanded, her face lined with anxiety. "Breakfast-time has been and gone long ago, and you haven't eaten a thing."

"We want to look for Phantom. We want you to take us out in the car," my brother said. "He must be somewhere."

10

We searched all morning, and again in the afternoon, until our eyes ached and Cousin Mary had no money left for petrol. Everywhere we stopped and asked people, "Have you seen a beautiful golden dun horse?" And all the time deep inside me I knew that we were wasting time because by now Phantom was across the sea, or locked up somewhere out of sight. We stopped at a police station while Cousin Mary went inside to enquire and Fiona said for the twentieth time, "I'm awful sorry, Jean. I feel so guilty. If only I could help."

Angus said, "It's all my fault, that's obvious, isn't it? If only I hadn't gone out on Peppermint none of it would have happened."

"We all know that *if only* are the saddest words in the English language," I replied.

"I think *too late* are even sadder," replied my brother. "But if no one minds about the beastly guns in the attic, why the kidnapping?"

"Because the police can't turn a blind eye if they are told about them," replied Fiona. "They must take action; it's a terrible situation that we are in."

Cousin Mary returned and I sat hating Ireland because it had taken Phantom from me. "Perhaps there will be a message for us at home," suggested Cousin Mary, looking at my miserable face. "The police have heard nothing of him, but they are going to look among the tinkers."

"The tinkers!" I cried. "They must be mad. He's hidden away somewhere. They should search every farm and stable, every turf cutter's shed, every ship."

"You think he's been stolen then?" inquired Cousin Mary.

"Yes."

Cousin Mary showed no surprise, probably she was beyond surprise by this time. Clouds were gathering in the sky promising more rain. "We must hear something soon. He can't just disappear for ever. People are very honest round here. Perhaps Father Paul will have heard something . . ."

Postcards of Nigeria waited for us in the hall. They seemed hopelessly out of date. *Wish you were here, too. We miss you. Lovely, exotic food. But horses here too thin for your liking. We saw a herd of elephants the day before yesterday.* Mine was of monkeys up a tree. It seemed irrelevant. What did I care for monkeys when I had lost Phantom? If only they would send a phone number, I thought. If I could just talk to Dad for a few minutes, just ask what we should do. The hills outside rumbled with thunder.

"They are all right. Swap?" said Angus.

There was an elephant on his postcard. *Wish you were both here*, it said. *Lots of singing, dancing and strange food. Hotel air-conditioned. Love.*

"I wanted a proper letter," I said. "Not a silly postcard." I stood staring out of the window at the darkening hills. Rain was falling now, bouncing off the rocks, lightning flashed, lighting up the gorse.

I started to pray for Phantom's return, silently, without moving my lips. I imagined him shut up somewhere listening to the thunder, the rain falling on a corrugated roof. Suddenly there seemed no hope any

86

more. Our parents would offer to buy me another horse. They would try to console me. But I didn't want another horse. I only wanted Phantom.

"You might help. We are all getting tea," exclaimed my brother. "Your foot can't be that bad."

I went on praying, hoping that the thunder would somehow help, that the lightning would suddenly reveal Phantom standing like a sentinel on the hilltop, almost as yellow as the gorse. But nothing happened; the rain simply fell harder, endless Irish rain. I didn't care about helping; they could manage well enough without me. Let them call me lazy. Nothing really mattered, not any more.

Cousin Mary pushed me into a chair. "You look awful," she said. "What's the matter now?"

"Nothing."

"Are you ill?"

"No."

"Does your foot hurt?"

"No."

I hated her. I knew it now, because she was all part of a country which had taken Phantom from me. I resolved to go to the police in the morning. I would hobble there alone and tell them everything, for nothing could ever be worse than it was now. Let them shoot Phantom. All right. But I would have revenge. I would see that the boy who kidnapped Angus and demanded money with menaces went to prison for years and years. And if Cousin Mary was put in prison for keeping ammunition in her attic, who cared? Not me. Donnie O'Reagan? Let him go too.

"You're crying," said Cousin Mary.

"I'm not."

"There are tears falling on your plate and you're not eating anything."

Suddenly I couldn't bear it any more. I rushed from

the room, banging my plaster on the door. I hobbled upstairs, slammed my bedroom door and stood staring outside, hating everything and everybody, wishing the whole gloomy, doom-laden house could go up in flames—ammunition and all. For an insane moment I even contemplated setting fire to it. Standing outside watching the flames and laughing hysterically.

"I've brought you a plate of cakes, sausage and bread and butter," said Angus, standing nervously in the doorway. "Do cheer up."

"Cheer up?" I shouted. "What's there to cheer up about? Tell me. Just tell me."

"While there's life there's hope," replied Angus, advancing with the plate. "If you eat, you'll feel better."

"I've always been afraid I would lose Phantom," I answered, taking a cake. "But not in this way; not miles from home. If I knew he was dead I could stop hoping. As it is, every time I hear a neigh I think it's him."

"It is always darkest before dawn," said Angus. "Have another sausage. Fiona is on our side now."

"I'm going to the police in the morning. I'm going to tell them everything. They can't let blackmail go unchecked. It's a terrible crime. Do you think it was really a bluff, that I could have got you back without trading Phantom for you?"

"I don't know. I think they need money. Perhaps they are being blackmailed. I think it is far more deadly than we ever imagined."

"And they really do kill people?"

"Yes."

"And everybody's frightened of them?"

"Yes."

Another day was ending. I had lost count of the days we had been in Ireland, but suddenly it seemed like eternity.

"One never thinks dreadful things will happen to

oneself," I said. "And when they do, it's an awful shock."

"We chose a bad moment to visit."

I stayed in my room for the rest of the evening, my face hideous from crying. Before I climbed into bed I heard shots coming from the hills and the cries of frightened birds. It was a very dark night and by midnight rain was falling in torrents from an ink-black sky. Cousin Mary and Fiona didn't come near me; probably they thought it better for me to grieve alone.

I didn't sleep. I listened to the big clock downstairs chime the hours, and each hour seemed to take away a little bit of hope. I was still awake when the first thin light of dawn pierced the night sky. In the distance cocks began to herald another day. It was then that I heard a noise which sounded like hoofs coming down the rough drive towards the house. I sat up and listened telling myself it was only my imagination, that it was simply the sound of rain falling on stones, that I had heard the noise simply because I had wanted to hear it for so long. But I climbed out of bed and found that I was shaking all over. Pulling back the curtains I looked out. I rubbed my eyes and stared and couldn't speak for the lump rising in my throat; then I shouted "Phantom!" He raised his head and neighed. The next moment I was running downstairs struggling with the bolts on the front door, throwing the door wide, charging out into the pouring rain—still in my pyjamas. Bits of rope hung from his fetlocks. Rain and sweat dripped from his golden coat.

"You've come back. In spite of everything . . ." He nuzzled my hair as I put my arm round his neck and he followed me to the stable. Only Peppermint was inside, but he welcomed us with a whinny.

"Come on, Phantom. I'll put you inside, then I'll put

on some clothes and rub you down and I'll give you the best feed you've ever had."

He followed me like a dog. I found the flashlight which hung in the stable, and now I could see how tucked up he was. He had lost a shoe and there was a sore on his head where he must have fought against a headcollar. I bolted the door and gave him a heap of hay, then hobbled indoors for dry clothes because, by now, my pyjamas were soaked through. All the time, over and over again, I kept thinking, he's come back, he's found his way back! And it seemed like a miracle as dawn rose slowly above the hills. I hurried upstairs and shook Angus.

"He's come back!" I cried. "Wake up. He's come back."

"What? Who?" said Angus, sitting up with his hair on end.

"Phantom!"

"You must be dreaming," cried Angus, sitting up.

"He's in the stable, soaking wet."

I put on jeans and a polo-necked jersey and Angus met me in the passage, still in his pyjamas.

"They may come after him," he said. "We need a gun."

"No, no guns, please," I replied quickly.

"They were shooting in the hills half the night. Perhaps they were shooting at him."

"No," I answered, for I didn't want to believe him, to listen to any more bad news. I just wanted to feed Phantom and be happy. "They were shooting at birds. I heard them screaming."

"No one shoots birds at night."

Phantom looked worse when I reached him. I put a rug on him inside out and fetched him water. I cut the bits of sad, tattered rope from his fetlocks. I fetched more peat and put it in his box, wishing for long golden straw, and all the time day was breaking outside. Angus appeared carrying a stick.

"There's no one about at present," he said. "But they will come, never fear." He ran his hands down Phantom's tendons and found a thorn.

"We must get a padlock for the door, and mount a guard day and night," he said.

"He's stopped shivering," I replied. "And he's eating. Couldn't we take him somewhere safe?"

"We haven't enough money," replied Angus. "But at least we can keep an eye on him here."

"They hobbled him," I said. "And kept him tied up."

"They must have been afraid he would jump out."

I fetched him a feed from where the food was kept.

"They won't come in daylight, will they?" I asked.

"I shouldn't think so," said Angus.

I was suddenly tired, tired and wonderfully happy at the same time. The nightmare's over—he's come back! We've won! I thought.

"I will stay with him while you go back to bed. You look most peculiar," Angus told me. "Your eyes have shrunk into the back of your head. And you should be resting your foot."

"You won't leave him, will you?"

Angus shook his head. "Not till Donnie O'Reagan takes over."

I went back across the yard to the house. Another day had come—a beautiful day with everything sparkling with rain. Fiona was looking out of her window.

"Phantom's back!" I shouted. "He's come back." I wanted to tell everyone, the whole world.

"Thanks be to God," she cried.

Donnie O'Reagan had sent for a vet. Phantom's temperature was 103. He stood shivering in spite of two rugs and a hot mash, resting his unshod hoof. He had lost half his mane, and looked a sorry sight in the light of midday.

"They couldn't keep him however hard they tried," said Donnie O'Reagan, with wonderment in his voice. "He found his way back here. What a horse!"

"Will he live?" I asked. "He's not going to die, is he?"

The vet had arrived. We heard the crunch of his car tyres outside on the gravel. He was a quiet man who called Phantom "My little darling," but none of it made any difference. Phantom was terrified of him. He stood on his hind legs and rushed round the box banging his head on the sides. I couldn't hold him and nor could Donnie O'Reagan, so at last we put a twitch on him, and he stood then as tense as a taut rope.

"What's been happening to him?" the vet asked. "He looks in awful bad shape."

"He's been lost on the hills, stolen by tinkers more than likely," replied Donnie O'Reagan.

"Or by the gangsters who live in these parts," said my brother in a loud voice. But the vet was a man of few words. He looked at me and asked, "Has he been like this before?"

I replied, "Yes, in Virginia, USA. He nearly died there one winter." I remembered the icicles hanging on the trees in the Blue Ridge Mountains and the long trek home.

"I thought so." The vet was listening to Phantom's heart. I saw myself never riding him again. I prepared myself to hear the fateful words. "His heart's finished."

"That's all right," said the vet putting the stethoscope away. "He'll live yet. We'll give him a shot of penicillin. His lungs are a bit dicey and there's quite a few crackles; but keep him warm, feed him well and he'll pull through."

Angus's eyes met mine. Phantom was going to be all

right. Everything would be back to normal. It was all I wanted at that moment.

The vet slipped the needle into Phantom's neck. We took off the twitch.

"Do you want to settle up now or at the end of the treatment?"

"At the end," replied my brother. "How long will he take to get well?"

"He should be better by tomorrow, but it will take him a month to be really well again. You won't be able to hunt him before November."

"I don't care about hunting. I just want him to live, and to be all right to ride in the end," I said.

Angus thanked the vet and shook him by the hand. He seemed very grown-up suddenly.

"And don't let him out on the hills again. They're wicked for a horse like him," said the vet.

"We've still got ten pounds and we can always borrow off Cousin Mary," said Angus. "But I think we'll have to stay up tonight, don't you? It would be awful if we lost him again. They might simply come and shoot him out of spite. They're quite mad."

Donnie O'Reagan was mixing Phantom another feed. I wondered for the first time who was meant to pay for all the feeds, the clean loose box, the endless hay nets bulging with hay—Mum and Dad, Cousin Mary, or me from my money in the Post Office at home?

"Lunch," called Fiona from the house. "Hurry up, it's roast chicken."

11

"You had better read this," said Cousin Mary, handing us the morning paper to read.

It told us that the kidnapped envoy had been released. "So you won't be with us much longer," Cousin Mary told us. "Poor Fiona. We will be so quiet without you."

"I'll be all right."

"The vet seems very sensible; he's coming again tomorrow. He thinks Phantom will recover." I put down the newspaper. I wished that our parents were with us already. "How long will it take them to come?"

"Who?"

"Mum and Dad."

"Oh, I don't know, dear; a day or two I expect."

It seemed literally years since we had parted. Even Aunt Nina seemed to have stayed with us a century ago. We started to wash up. "I expect they'll fly to Dublin, hire a car and come straight down. It's years since I've seen either of them," continued Cousin Mary, washing a plate. "I expect they've aged. We all have."

"Mum is still all right; but Dad's a bit careworn, you know, crow's feet round his eyes, that sort of thing," replied Angus.

"I hope they don't go home first," I said.

"I expect they'll bring you back lots of knick-knacks and African shirts. I must get some whiskey in for your father," said Cousin Mary hanging up the dishcloth.

After the lunch things were washed up and put away we drank great mugs of coffee, sitting in the chairs in the hall. Cousin Mary told us about her youth; about hunt balls and dancing all night long, and how the men wore scarlet coats, also how there was soup and bacon and eggs before you went home at four in the morning. I thought how sad it was that we all grow older. "But Fiona won't have anything of that if she's going to be a nun," she finished.

Fiona looked out of the window. I never knew what she saw there; most likely only what was in her mind at the moment; perhaps herself dressed as a nun. Certainly the rough grass wasn't interesting.

"I want peace," she said. "I'm tired of the killing which is always going on everywhere. I want to forget it."

"Why don't you come and stay with us?" Angus asked.

"If Mum doesn't mind."

But now there was a rapping at the door and we found Donnie O'Reagan outside saying, "You had better come quick. Phantom's down. I'm afraid he'll twist a gut. I can't get him up on my own."

I forgot my foot in plaster, and ran with the others, cursing myself for ever leaving Phantom. He was kicking against the partition, making a terrible noise. He was soaked in sweat. His tattered mane clung to his neck and his sides were spattered with peat. Angus hit him, while I pulled, talking to him all the time, saying over and over again, "Phantom, get up. Stand up, come on, move." And all the time my heart was beating against my side like a piston engine and I was imagining the end again—Phantom dead.

"I'll get a drench." Phantom was standing up, his wet sides going in and out like bellows, his eyes waiting for the next spasm of pain.

Donnie O'Reagan came back with a bottle. He stood on a box and held Phantom's tongue. "Hold him still whatever you do." Half of it went down his arm. It smelt of turpentine or linseed, I couldn't tell which.

"He'll need an enema. Will you be calling the vet?" Cousin Mary left us silently.

"If he's not better in twenty minutes I'll give him another drench," said Donnie O'Reagan wiping his arms with a towel. "I'll just be getting some soapy water. Keep him up. Walk him up and down. He mustn't roll."

"OK," said Angus.

I couldn't speak. It was as though suddenly my throat was paralysed. I could hear Fiona sniffing. Angus hit Phantom as I led him outside. He tried to go down just outside the door on the concrete. "Hit him," shouted Donnie O'Reagan running towards his house. "He mustn't go down. If he goes down we're lost."

I knew what he meant. Once a horse has twisted a gut, nothing can be done. He'll die in agony. He may have twisted it already, I thought. Why did I leave him for lunch?

"I can't get hold of the vet," said Cousin Mary, coming back. "Is he any better?"

The sweat from Phantom's neck was all over my arms. I was struggling with him all the time now. "I can't hold him much longer," I cried.

"Let me try," Angus said. "I'll hold him up on the other side."

"Keep him walking, Donnie said you were to keep him walking," shouted Fiona.

"Can't you get another vet?" I cried. "Is there only one vet in the whole of Ireland?"

"He has to boil a kettle," said Fiona. "He has no hot water in the cottage."

96

"I was talking about vets," I screamed. "Stand up, will you, Phantom?"

He was down again on some old cobbles. "Don't let him roll," screamed Angus.

"Hit him," I yelled. "Stick some scissors in him. Anything."

Angus hit him with a rope. I pulled. My hands were bleeding now. "Get up," I yelled. "Phantom. Please get up . . . Up . . . Up . . . Phantom up . . ."

He stood up slowly shaking all over, his eyes were still glassy but some light was coming back to them, some sort of animal sanity at last. He looked at me as though he saw me for the first time and his ears went forward, and suddenly I wanted to cry.

Donnie O'Reagan was coming towards us now with a bucket with a rubber syringe in it. "It's over, the spasm's over," he said.

"Thanks be to God," said Fiona, wiping her eyes.

It was as though he was coming back from a long journey. He nuzzled my pockets and then wiped his head on my shirt.

"We fed him too well, too soon. I'll be getting him a hot mash with some salts in it. He won't be needing the enema now."

"Do you still want a vet?"

"Not now."

"You've saved his life," I said. "If you hadn't found him he would have twisted a gut by now."

Donnie O'Reagan shook his head. "It was God's will," he said. "It was a pity we ever left him though, we should have stayed."

"I shan't leave him again," I answered. "Not day or night. I swear it now; not till he's really well and we're home again."

"But you can't eat and sleep out here, and the stable is full of spiders," cried Fiona.

"I will be with her," said Angus. "We can't risk Phantom's life again."

I was leading him up and down the yard now. He walked like an old horse with his head hanging down. Angus put his rug straight. "He looks awful, only fit for the knackers," he said.

"Shut up. He's going to recover. He's going to jump at Wembley next year," I answered. "Aren't you, Phantom?"

"You are all filthy. If only you could see yourselves," said Cousin Mary.

"I don't want to, and I like being filthy," I answered rudely. I could gladly bury myself in coal-dust if it would make Phantom well.

"You must look better when your parents arrive."

"They don't care how we look."

I put Phantom back in his box. Donnie O'Reagan brought him a hot mash. Somewhere far away a clock chimed four times.

"I'll wash, then I'll take over while you clean yourself up," said Angus, who had just begun to care how he looked, to demand spotted shirts and leather jackets.

"I will be taking my wife to the hospital to see little Neil," said Donnie O'Reagan. "I will not be long. Here is a second drench if he needs it."

The bottle was covered with cobwebs. It looked as though it had lain on a shelf for years. I thanked Donnie O'Reagan and watched him leave; I thought, there goes a real friend.

"I will bring you something to eat. There are some sleeping-bags in mother's bedroom," said Fiona. "And I'll find you a lantern. I would stay with you tonight, but I can't stand the spiders, truly I can't."

"How funny, I always look on them as friends. Mum calls them 'brothers'," I said.

"I always was scared of them."

98

I was alone with Phantom now. He ate his mash slowly and his ears were still damp with sweat. I brushed his mane until Angus appeared and said, "Your turn to wash now. You smell of drench and sick horse."

"You're going to be well now," I told Phantom. "We're going to watch you day and night until we go home."

I thought of home as I walked indoors and England seemed the most civilised country on earth. I hope Dad doesn't get another posting for years and years, I thought, washing in the old-fashioned cloakroom where the taps were made of brass and the window-panes were green with a pattern on them.

Fiona gave me two sleeping-bags. "They're a bit moth-eaten," she said. They were khaki with tapes down the side. They looked at least one hundred years old.

I told Cousin Mary that we were staying with Phantom. "He's too sick to be left," I said firmly. "He might have another attack of colic at any time."

She shrugged her shoulders. Wisps of her hair had come unpinned as she sat brushing Connelly. "Wrap yourselves up well," she said.

Fiona found us an old lantern with a wick, which she filled with paraffin. It smelt rather, but it gave out a lovely warm comforting light, quite different from that of a torch.

"I'll just be fetching you some more matches," she said.

"We won't need them for hours," I said.

"Darkness comes soon. The nights are drawing in, to be sure. And I have to be going to church tonight. There's a special service. It's a saint's day, you understand."

Angus and I made ourselves hay beds in the passage

99

outside the loose boxes. The big grey horse and Peppermint were leaning over their doors and blowing warm air from their nostrils. Phantom stood at the back of his box resting a hind leg. Horses can sleep standing up, and his eyes were shut—so I think he was sleeping.

Fiona appeared with mugs of tea and a plate of sandwiches.

"I'll bring you supper when I return from church. Something hot."

"You're an angel," replied Angus.

"Can't one of us get it for ourselves?" I asked.

"No, I'll bring it." She was dressed ready for church.

"I feel a heathen," Angus muttered. "When did we last go to church?"

"Years ago."

"Exactly."

"I'll go and get some books," said Angus presently. "Something light and easy to read."

"Something about horses."

A mist was coming down outside. It was a drowsy sort of evening. If I had shut my eyes I would have fallen asleep.

"There's only this old book about horses," said Angus returning. "I'm sorry."

It was the one I had looked at once before. It was full of men in top hats delivering foals; and for nearly every illness horses were bled, preferably with leeches. Angus had found a book by Hammond Innes. Whenever I spoke he said, "Shut up, this is exciting," or "Ssh." In the end I fetched a body brush and groomed Phantom. Presently Fiona appeared with scrambled eggs on toast on tin plates. "Here's a Thermos too, with hot coffee in it and two mugs."

The mugs and the tin plates looked as though they had been through several wars along with the sleeping-bags. But the Thermos was Cousin Mary's and quite new. "I've brought a bag of apples too."

Fiona waited while we ate. "The telephone is working again. It was cut off because we didn't pay the bill."

"We must owe you lots of money," said Angus, handing her his empty plate. "I hope we are paying guests."

"I don't know to be sure, but you're very welcome."

"Can't we wash up our plates?"

"Whatever will you be saying next?" asked Fiona. "Where would you be washing them now?"

"In the horses' buckets."

Angus lit the lantern. "We mustn't kick it over, or the whole stable will go up like a tinderbox," he said.

I went to look at Phantom. He was eating hay and looked better. His ears were warm at last, and his sides were beginning to fill out.

Angus returned to his reading. The sky grew dark outside. We went indoors in turn to clean our teeth and put on pyjamas under riding coats. Cousin Mary had already gone to bed with a headache, and the dogs, which slept in her room, had gone too. Fiona was waiting to lock up the house. "Mother insists on it," she said. "Though I hate locking you out."

"It doesn't matter; we'll yell if we want anything," I answered. "Don't worry."

"I hope Phantom's all right."

"Of course he is," I said touching wood.

Angus read for hours by lantern light. Birds fluttered in trees; once I heard apples fall from the trees in Donnie O'Reagan's garden. Angus was wearing his watch. At eleven o'clock Phantom lay down. It was completely dark now, but neither of us was frightened or even nervous. I think we both felt at home with the smell of horse all about us. Angus bolted the stable door on the inside; usually it was never shut in the summer. I took a last look at Phantom by lantern light. He looked sweet lying in his rug, and the long flannel leg bandages which Donnie O'Reagan insisted on him wearing. I sat with him, my arms round his neck, until Angus called, "Come on, for goodness sake, there won't be any paraffin left in the lantern if we keep it alight much longer."

"I wish we could always sleep in here," I said, getting into my sleeping-bag. "It's much more peaceful than the house."

"Until the mice start to squeak," replied Angus. "And the spiders start to crawl."

"Phantom really is better. I hope he stays well now for ever and ever."

"So do I. He's caused enough trouble."

"You're a nice one to talk."

"What do you mean?"

"I mean you started it all by going into the attic when you were told not to. If you had done what you were told you would never have been kidnapped."

"That's what you think."

"And it hasn't done any good; the stuff's still there," I added. "So it was all in vain."

"Are you trying to pick a quarrel?" asked Angus.

"No. But you were being beastly about Phantom."

"Listen," said Angus.

"You're imagining things," I answered. "It's just a plane flying overhead."

"That's what you think," replied Angus, getting out of his sleeping-bag and feeling for his shoes in the dark. "But I think it is something else. I think we are going to have visitors."

My inside had started to flutter in a funny way. I sat up in the dark. The noise was still there. It was the sound of an engine running and then the sound of feet in boots on gravel, which made my hair stand on end.

Then I was out of my sleeping-bag too, finding my one wellington boot, which had a sock inside that I didn't bother to put on. We didn't speak, because suddenly there seemed no need for words. But I knew somehow that Angus had taken a gun out of the pile of hay and was dusting it. Then I heard him pull something back and load, and cock it ready to fire. I remembered that he had learnt to shoot long ago when we still went to boarding school. I stood up and fetched a fork from the end of the stable and waited, wishing that there was more light, or that we could light the lantern.

The engine had stopped running; but there was still the sound of hurrying feet and I felt as though I had been waiting my whole life for this moment.

12

The voices outside were soft and Irish.

"We shouldn't be leaving the horse," said one.

"I wouldn't be beat by a slip of a girl," said another.

"We have to keep to our word," argued a third.

"Let him be. That's all I'm saying. Let her keep him."
I could feel the tenseness in Angus now, as he stood
waiting with the gun.

"Don't shoot anyone," I whispered. "Just frighten
them a bit."

"Shut up," he hissed.

The horses were listening too. It was as though we
were all waiting to see what fate had ready for us. I held
on to the fork. Far away an owl hooted.

"We will be taking him further away this time.
There's a gentleman that's coming from the United
States. He's looking for a dressage horse, you know.
We can ask a lot if he's in good shape . . . Two thousand
or more, and that will be buying a lot of guns."

We heard the boots come nearer. A hand rattled the
doors. "It's been bolted on the inside, now how's that?"

"I wouldn't be knowing."

"Would they be expecting us then?"

"It could be locked. O'Reagan could have the key up
at his cottage."

"We had best be moving the ammunition soon, if it's
to be shipped out tomorrow night."

"We had best be seeing the little horse first. I have the van for him parked down the road."

"Get a pole then and we'll ram the door."

I was just behind Angus now. My throat had gone dry. "Keep back," he whispered. "The gun will kick a bit—I won't hurt anyone. Get back."

There was a gap between the door and the doorpost. He was going to fire through it. I prayed that he wouldn't hurt anyone; that somehow we would all come through unscathed; but at that moment it didn't seem possible. We seemed to have reached the end of a long struggle, which had started when we first put a foot in the attics.

"Put a headcollar on Phantom. If they break down the door, gallop through it. Hurry," whispered Angus.

"What about you?"

"I'll be all right."

I opened Phantom's door and slipped a hemp halter over his head. I knotted the rope on the other side so that I had reins, and vaulted on.

They started to batter the door. Angus fired. Outside someone shouted. Then shots started to come into the stable and Angus ducked sideways, shouting, "Are you ready?"

"Jump up behind," I shouted.

"I can't," he shouted. "You go."

Men were coming in now, shouting, "It would never be Donnie O'Reagan shooting like that."

I rode Phantom straight at them, out through the door, and saw that the lights were on in the house and in Donnie O'Reagan's cottage too.

I banged my knee on the doorpost as Phantom jumped what was left of the door lying outside in the yard. There seemed to be people everywhere. I thought I heard Fiona calling and Donnie O'Reagan shouting to one of his children to come back. I wasn't afraid of being shot but I was afraid for Angus still in the stable. Then the shooting started up again. I rode Phantom at the wall which separated the yard from the paddock. I felt his hindlegs go under him and his ears went forward and then we were over, galloping to the far side of the house where we would be safe.

Fiona flung open a window and yelled, "Is Angus all right?"

"No. He's trapped in the stable. He needs help," I yelled back, and as I spoke my blood started to run cold, so that suddenly I was shivering and my teeth started to chatter. I wished I was with Angus now in the stable, standing beside him shoulder to shoulder, for what was the use of saving Phantom and losing Angus? I thought of all the times we had quarrelled and all the good times we had shared together. I thought that if I went back to the yard, the men might start shooting at me and Phantom, and give Angus a chance to escape. I turned Phantom and rode him at the wall; but this time he refused, which wasn't surprising since it was more than four feet high. I shouted at him and tried again. Now the shooting had started up once more and I saw Donnie O'Reagan standing outside his cottage yelling, "Leave the kid alone. He's only a youngster!"

I wondered why Cousin Mary hadn't come out to help; then I remembered the sleeping-pill she had taken and imagined her sleeping peacefully while we struggled almost alone outside. The stable seemed full of men now and someone had turned on the lights of the Land Rovers. I kicked Phantom as hard as I could and rode again at the wall. This time he went over, and now I stood in the yard shouting, "Leave my brother alone. You can have my horse, but leave him alone."

Then I saw Angus was still free, crawling along the stable roof. I rode nearer and called, "Jump, for goodness sake, jump! Phantom will carry us both." But by now there were two Land Rovers in the yard blocking both the wall and the entrance, and I realised that I was trapped, that there was no way out at all. I looked at the Irish faces all around me and they looked nice enough. It seemed silly that we had to be enemies when we spoke almost the same language and looked just the same. My teeth had stopped chattering and my head felt completely clear. I saw everything as though I was seeing it for the first and the last time. I imagined my own funeral. My parents laying a wreath on my coffin and the Prime Minister of England seeing the Prime Minister of Eire. I saw the newspapers with their screaming headlines: *English Children Shot in Cold Blood* and *Cold-blooded Murder of Holiday Children*. I also felt silly in my pyjamas with my one wellington boot.

Angus had slid down from the roof by this time. He had torn his pyjama jacket and lost his gun. He looked at me and muttered, "This is the end. Why didn't you gallop away across the hills?"

I don't know what the Irishmen would have done if we hadn't been interrupted. They looked embarrassed and undecided, and I don't think they wanted to kill us. But unexpectedly, there were cars now blocking the drive and out of them policemen streamed like angry bees from a hive; and the men started to run in all directions, leaping into their Land Rovers, starting the engines, running towards the hills, shouting things to one another in Gaelic. But they were too late. All the escape routes were blocked and the policemen called to them by name. "O'Connelly, come over here. Sean O'Flatery, and what do you think you're doing?" They slowly collected like a shame-faced pack of hounds and started to excuse themselves. "I was doing nothing for sure," they said, and, "It was a night out we were having," and "It's a funny thing, when you'll be spoiling a saint's day celebration for sure."

Then we saw Fiona coming towards us. Her face was red from crying.

"Who sent for the police?" asked my brother, but suddenly we knew. We could see it in her face as she looked at us.

"I thought they were killing you, Angus," she said. "I couldn't have you killed. But they are my father's friends, you understand. It was a terrible decision. Now I don't know what will happen for sure, for there's explosives and all in the attic. And my father will never speak to me again, that's certain, for he's a funny man if ever there was one."

Angus put an arm round her shoulder. "Thank you. Thank you very much," he said.

It wasn't enough of course, nothing would ever be enough in return for what she had done. The police were carrying ammunition and explosives from the attic now. Dawn had come all warm and rosy with a smell of damp leaves, dew-drenched grass, and threads finer than silk hanging on the bushes along the drive.

I dismounted and Donnie O'Reagan said, "You had best be putting your little horse in the paddock now. The stable's full of bullets and we wouldn't want him swallowing one in his hay."

He looked small and defeated and presently the police led him away. I wanted to cry. "Not him. He's all right."

Fiona was crying and none of us knew what to do. The Irishmen were put into trucks and driven away. An Inspector told us that he would be wanting to talk to us all in the big house as soon as we were washed and dressed. Suddenly it was another day. Phantom rolled over and over in the grass. Angus said, "Don't worry, he's too tired to jump out for a bit."

108

"We had better tell Mother," Fiona said in a miserable voice. "She must be still asleep and will be getting a terrible shock, if we don't prepare her."

"I wish we could pay you back somehow," Angus told her.

"You can't wipe out the past, however much you try," said Fiona. "My father's been found out and that's a truly terrible thing."

My foot in plaster, with its sock, was soaking wet. My toes ached. The front door was unlocked. The dogs greeted us and, to my surprise, the post had been delivered as usual.

"They'll all hate me now, truly they will. That was Mrs O'Flatery's son they led away. I betrayed him," said Fiona.

Angus and I looked at one another and could think of nothing to say. "I'll give you all my money if that'll help," I offered. "I won a bet with a rich American last year so I've got quite a lot. You could give it to Mrs O'Flatery in compensation for the loss of her son."

"I will give you the money that Dad was going to spend on a horse for me," offered Angus. "It's at least a thousand pounds."

"I don't want money. It would only buy more guns, and that would mean more trouble," replied Fiona wearily, as though we were two tiresome children and she was our grandmother.

The dogs welcomed us with excited barks.

"I shot one of the men," said Angus. "I hit him in the foot, and I got a graze on my arm." I saw the blood on his pyjamas for the first time and I thought, however tiresome he is, he's brave, braver than I shall ever be.

"We had better bathe it or something. Does it hurt?" I asked.

"Not much, though it felt terrible when it happened. It's only a flesh wound anyway; nothing to fuss over," replied Angus, as though he was now an experienced soldier. "I like fighting actually. I think I will try for Welbeck College, if I've got the right exam results."

"Welbeck College!"

"It's the Army college; it gets you in somehow or other," said Angus vaguely, and I suddenly saw that he was sagging at the knees.

"Put your head down," I shouted. "Put it between your knees."

Fiona had gone into the house ahead of us. Upstairs she and Cousin Mary were having a tremendous argument. The police were in the sitting-room and the sun was shining through the windows, showing up the dust and cobwebs which Mrs O'Flatery never got round to.

"But calling the police, that was going too far. Why didn't you wake me?" cried Cousin Mary. "Now heaven knows what will happen."

"Ssh, Mother; they are in the drawing-room."

"I could have dealt with them."

"They were killing Angus. Shooting him to death in the stable. Did you want him murdered, Mother?"

I had pushed Angus's head between his knees and slowly the colour came back into his face. He said, "I must have fainted. How silly and feeble."

"You had better come upstairs and show it to Cousin Mary," I replied taking his arm. "You don't want tetanus and you will certainly need an injection and lots of antiseptic. There may be a bullet still in it."

"I wish they had never visited us," said Cousin Mary, unaware of our presence in the hall. "They've been a bother from start to finish and as for Jean, she thinks of nothing but riding."

"I like them, Mother," said Fiona. "Angus is the nicest person I've ever met. Truly he is. He's brave and kind and not selfish at all."

"Wow!" I whispered in Angus's ear. "Did you hear that?"

"Shut up. You can't be beastly about someone who has just saved your life. Anyway, I like being admired. It does my ego good," replied Angus.

We started to climb the stairs together and then he fainted again. Cousin Mary came rushing down, saying, "He's bleeding all over the carpet."

Fiona cried, "Mother, stop bothering about the carpet; he'll bleed to death in a minute."

We carried him into his room where Cousin Mary applied pressure with a large wad of cotton wool, and presently the bleeding stopped.

"I must have fainted again, how silly," said Angus sitting up.

"Lie down at once," replied Cousin Mary. "Fetch him some water, Fiona. Don't just stand like an idiot— you children will be the death of us all. Everything was all right till you came."

"You asked us," replied Angus in a faint voice.

"You are wanted downstairs, Madam," said Donnie O'Reagan's voice through the door.

"We'll be needing the doctor," said Fiona, returning with some water. "Angus can't be questioned."

"Will I have to see the police by myself then?" I asked, but no one answered. Suddenly everything seemed too big for me to manage. For how could I explain everything, tell all, without making Cousin Mary or Fiona sound guilty? Would they believe me? Would anyone? Wasn't the whole tale too unlikely, too fantastic? I couldn't believe any of it had really happened myself now that it was over, so how could I convince anyone else? I wished that I was wounded and would faint like Angus. I wanted to run away to Donnie O'Reagan's cottage and hide myself among his children.

"I can go downstairs," said Angus. "I'm all right."

"Your wound will bleed if you move," replied Fiona. "If they *must* question you, they can come up here."

Cousin Mary had gone. There were still three police cars parked outside in the drive. It was a perfect summer day. Leaning out of Angus's window I could hear bees buzzing among the flowers.

"You had better dress," said Angus. "You really are disgusting to look at. Your plaster is covered with horse dung, your face is filthy and there's blood all down the front of your pyjamas."

I didn't answer. I could see a vehicle coming along the drive, and it wasn't a police car. It looked like a Dormobile with two people in front waving—a man and a woman.

"There's more visitors," I said. "They look like guests."

"What a moment to come," cried my brother.

"No one is expected," said Fiona.

They were coming nearer now and I started to jump up and down yelling, "It's Mum and Dad . . . They're here."

"Let me see," said Angus in a funny hoarse voice. "Get out of the way, Fiona."

"Don't," I cried, "You'll only faint again." I ran along the passage, down the stairs, across the hall, through the wide-open door. I could hear the police talking in the big sitting-room and there was one standing in the hall who said, "And where will you be going, Miss?"

"Just outside," I cried. "I won't be long."

Dad jumped out of the Dormobile first. "What's going on?" he yelled. "We've been stopped three times by the police!"

"What's happened to you, Jean? And where's Angus? Is Angus all right?" cried Mum.

112

"He's been shot, but he's all right," I said, trying to keep my voice steady, to sound normal and comforting.

"Shot?" Mum gasped. "Is he in hospital?"

"It's only a flesh wound," I answered. "He's upstairs in bed."

"You look awful," said Dad. "What's the matter with your foot?"

"It's getting better. We're all right," I answered, staring into their faces. "We're all right, honestly, quite all right. Oh, it's all such a long story. I lost Phantom. They took him."

"They?" asked Dad.

"There's blood all down your pyjamas," said Mum.

"I was just going to change." Everything was getting jumbled up; my voice seemed to come from a long way off. Mum and Dad receded into the distance. "I was just going to change. It's Angus's blood," I muttered. "I have to see the police. I don't know what to say . . ." My parents seemed to be coming back from a long way off. "She nearly fainted," said Mum.

"I'm going to get to the bottom of this. And *I'm* going to ask the questions," cried Dad, picking me up in his arms. "I am not having you bullied by a bunch of policemen."

"But you don't know what happened."

"Well, if you have to be questioned, you'll be clean and in bed. Not like you are now."

At last I knew that I was safe, that the grown-ups were taking over.

"Where's Angus's bedroom?" cried Mum, running ahead of us up the stairs.

It was like clambering into a safe cave after being hunted. I knew no one would hurt us now, that Dad and Mum would sort out everything.

"You came just in time," I said. "I'm not very good

113

with policemen and I didn't want to get Cousin Mary and Fiona into trouble; but now you can tell me what to say."

13

I was clean and washed and in bed at last.

"Begin at the beginning," said Dad.

"I don't know where it all began," I answered, "but I'll begin at the attics." There were two policemen in the room and one had a typewriter. A doctor had arrived and was attending to Angus in the next room. Dad had talked to Angus and knew about the gun and the shooting. In fact he knew almost everything.

"We shouldn't have gone in the attics, I can see that now," I began. Everything came back to me and I could see the boxes again and Fiona standing in the doorway in her nightie.

When I had finished Dad went outside with the two policemen. My toes were aching and I felt very sleepy, which was hardly surprising since I hadn't slept all night. Dad returned bearing a tray with a chop, three vegetables and a tall glass full of orange squash.

"Will Cousin Mary go to prison?" I asked. "And what about Fiona? I don't think they are bad at all, do you? Just victims of circumstances."

"Cousin Mary turned a blind eye like Nelson. I don't know what the law is about harbouring guns and explosives. Perhaps there isn't one. But either way I think she's going to get off scot-free. After all, she slept through everything, though whether by design or accident I don't know; and you can't punish an intimidated child. Fiona's been through a terrible time. She knew about the ammunition and explosives in the attics and she burned your letter to us, because she was afraid. She's younger than you are and I think she's been very brave; her father is the real villain of the piece. But of course Angus shouldn't have used a gun, and he fired first."

I ate my chop and three veg and asked after Phantom. Dad said that he was all right and stuffing himself with grass. He told me that the police were leaving and that he had a surprise for me and Angus, but that he would not tell me about till later. Fiona appeared then with some ice-cream. She looked like a small hunted animal and I felt very sorry for her, knowing that she was blaming herself for everything.

But great waves of exhaustion were sweeping over me now and I found difficulty in keeping my eyes open any longer. I ate my ice-cream, then muttering, "Thank you," collapsed in bed and without another thought I fell asleep, to dream of nothing, while outside afternoon turned to evening.

Everybody seemed to be in my room when I wakened.

"This is a council of war," said my brother.

"Not war, peace," answered Mum quickly.

"How is your foot, Jean? I think you will need a new plaster."

"The plaster's rather loose; I think it's cracked, but otherwise it's all right," I replied, rubbing the sleep from my eyes. "Why are you all here?"

"Dad has some good news," said Angus, who was wearing his arm in a sling. "We've all been waiting for you to wake up."

Cousin Mary sat a little apart from the others. I wondered whether she was still angry with me and

Angus. She sat on the edge of her chair with her hands in her lap. "What about Donnie O'Reagan?" I asked.

"He's all right. He's looking after Phantom. We are all going to see him in a minute," replied Dad.

"We must owe him lots of money," I said.

"It's really good news," said Mum. "I won some money with my Premium Bonds, so we're going to try and buy a Land Rover and trailer, plus a horse for Angus—and all drive back together."

I sat up in bed. "A Land Rover and trailer?" I cried. "So that we can go to lots of shows, and hunt. And we can go? We aren't going to prison or anything?"

"That's right," replied Dad. "I've been through everything with the police and since we aren't going to bring any charges against anyone, we can leave when we like."

"Donnie O'Reagan's got a fantastic grey," said Angus, and then stopped.

"He's super," I continued, "but terribly expensive."

"We'll look at him anyway," replied Mum. "You see the prize was very large—ten thousand pounds in fact."

"Ten thousand pounds!" exclaimed Angus.

"It's the first time I've ever won anything," said Mum.

"I want to dress and see Phantom," I said.

"Also Cousin Mary and Fiona are coming back with us for a holiday," continued Dad. "We hope to leave tomorrow."

Fiona was staring at Angus and Angus's eyes had gone glassy. (He told me afterwards that he was imagining himself hunting Donnie O'Reagan's grey at that moment.) Everyone left my room and, while I dressed, I digested the news that I had heard. I hoped we would buy a proper trailer with a roof and groom's compartment with a little door. I put on a polo-necked jersey and the jeans which Cousin Mary had slit at the bottom, so that they would fit over my plaster easily. I stared at the view outside and imagined the house empty and wondered what would become of Sean and Connie.

I found everyone waiting for me outside on the weedy gravel. It was one of those beautiful Irish evenings with the hills all blue in the distance and the grass greener than any grass I've ever seen. A sort of melancholy peace hung over everything.

Phantom was still grazing; he looked better already.

"The vet came when you were asleep," Dad told me. "He isn't coming again. He says he's cured himself."

Donnie O'Reagan was weeding his vegetable garden.

"You kids look at Phantom while we talk," said Dad.

"I'm not a kid," said Angus.

"Young people then."

The grey was in the stable. Angus went straight to him. "He's rather big," he said. "But I'm sure to grow, and I know he'll be good across country because I've seen Donnie lunging him over banks and walls; he's got the most marvellous scope and Donnie says he's as clever as a cat."

I put my arm round Phantom's neck. He looked very beautiful. "We'll soon be home," I told him. "You'll see Twilight again and the orchard will be full of apples."

Donnie O'Reagan was coming towards us with a saddle and bridle. "A babe in arms could ride him you know," he said.

Angus mounted the grey off a mounting block. He could only ride in one hand so he didn't jump, but he cantered circles and reined back and he kept stopping to call, "He's absolutely super."

"He's big enough," said Mum.

"Just right," replied Donnie O'Reagan. "I will sell him cheap to you. I don't want to make any profit, not after what's happened. He's two thousand to you."

"He's the best horse I've ever ridden," announced Angus halting in front of us. "There's so much in front

118

and such power behind. He's fantastic." He slid to the ground. "But he's awfully expensive," he added, "so I think we ought to look at some more horses. I don't want you to spend all your money on me."

But Mum was already writing in her cheque-book. "Two thousand is little enough nowadays, and I can never repay you for all you've done for Angus and Jean—you've been marvellous," she said.

"And now we need a Land Rover and a trailer," said Dad when Mum had put away her cheque-book, as though buying such things was a daily occurrence.

So everything seemed settled at last. Donnie O'Reagan was to look after the big house while Cousin Mary and Fiona stayed with us. Mum and Dad were to leave immediately to inspect Land Rovers at a garage which dealt in them. I was to go to the hospital in the morning to have my foot re-plastered. Our visit to Ireland was almost over. Angus and I sat in the garden and talked.

"In spite of everything I'm glad we came," said Angus. "It's been an adventure, and it isn't easy to have adventures nowadays."

"Where did you get the gun from?" I asked. "The one you fired?"

"From the cupboard under the stairs. It's only meant for shooting birds."

"Do you think they'll go to prison?" I asked next.

"For a few weeks or months I expect," said Angus.

"It's so lovely here," I said, gazing at the hills. "I would like to stay just a few more days."

"No thank you," said Angus, looking at his wounded arm.

"Lots of people come year after year, and nothing ever happens."

"They don't land in a hornet's nest like us," replied Angus.

119

We went indoors and packed. Fiona and Cousin Mary were turning out all the cupboards. Fiona had never left home before and Cousin Mary had not been away for twenty years, so it was quite an undertaking.

"I expect I shall have to sleep in the summer-house again or there won't be room, but I don't mind. I shall get up early and ride my grey before the flies are a nuisance," said Angus. "I'm going to call him Killarney because he's Irish . . . and beautiful."

Mum and Dad returned in the dark with a second-hand Land Rover and trailer. "Everything's so easy if you've got money," said Mum. "It's quite incredible the difference it makes."

They ate dinner with Cousin Mary in the dining-room, and Dad had brought two bottles of wine. After-wards Mum said that Cousin Mary had told them all her darkest secrets.

Next morning Mum drove me to the hospital. The doctor tutted over my plaster and said that I had been doing too much. I told him that it was the fault of gunmen who had kidnapped my brother and then stolen my pony. He gave me a funny look; I think he thought I was mad. Then he said, "You horsy girls can never stay either in one piece or one place." And I couldn't think of an answer.

The sun was shining when we went outside again. It was lovely to be driving about with Mum after so long.

"The garage is going to collect this vehicle," said Mum, changing gear at the traffic-lights. "We hired a Dormobile because we thought you might enjoy a little camping holiday, but finding you in such a state we've decided it would be better to go straight home."

I thought of Angus and myself riding down the leafy lanes of Oxfordshire and was inclined to agree.

When we got back there was a pile of suitcases outside the front door and Dad was looking harassed.

"We can put some in the groom's compartment," Angus was saying.

"We are going to catch the night boat," said Dad. "There's no time for discussion. Put them where you like."

"My saddle! I haven't got any tack. They kept it," I cried.

"We'll talk about that later," Dad said.

"But . . ."

"No buts," replied Dad.

Mrs O'Flatery was scurrying about like a demented hen talking about her son. "I always said it would be so; that the blessed Lord would punish him, but he wouldn't heed me," she said.

The trailer was attached to the Land Rover. Donnie O'Reagan was bandaging Killarney's legs.

"It's lucky there's room on the boat for us all; it's only because it's rained such a lot that some people have gone home early," said Dad.

Cousin Mary was frantically transferring clothes from one suitcase to another. Donnie O'Reagan put half a bale of hay, a bucket of feed and some water in the front of the trailer. Mrs O'Flatery handed round a plate of beef sandwiches and cups of instant coffee.

Phantom was ready, rugged and bandaged. "The police found his saddle and bridle in one of the Land Rovers," said Donnie O'Reagan.

"Oh, thank you, thank you very much."

"It is nothing at all," he said stacking, it into our Land Rover.

I led Phantom up the ramp into our beautiful trailer and suddenly I wanted to cry with joy, because we had survived and because now we had everything we had ever wanted.

Angus led Killarney in. Donnie O'Reagan threw up the ramp behind us. The Land Rover was loaded now.

"I'll look after the dogs like my own children," said Donnie O'Reagan.

Fiona had her arms round Connie.

"Remember to cancel the milk, O'Reagan," said Cousin Mary.

"I will look after everything."

"It's been a terrible week, I never want to see the like of it again," said Mrs O'Flatery, "and look at your poor children."

"You can't live without scars of some sort or other," said Dad, starting up the engine.

I looked at the house for the last time. Donnie O'Reagan stood waving, surrounded by dogs and children. Mrs O'Flatery waved a duster, calling "God bless you all."

I thought, soon it will seem like a dream, but we will have our scars to remind us. We could hear the horses moving about behind us in the trailer. Angus started talking to Fiona, trying to cheer her up. I hoped that we would get on all right together in Sparrow Cottage, and that the front door mat would be covered with envelopes for me filled with show schedules, when eventually we arrived home.

Angus started to talk about Killarney, about all his plans, and the future seemed full of joy and sunshine. I hoped that Fiona would enjoy it too.

Then out of the blue he said, "I'll come back one day. I'll hunt Killarney over the banks. In spite of everything, I love it here."

I said, "Me too."

"It has a magic," said Fiona, "which keeps calling you back. Have you read Yeats's poems?"

"Yes, The Lake Isle of Innisfree," said Angus. "But you will like England too, and perhaps you will take to riding—who knows?"

They talked to one another about school, and I sat

making plans, the same endless plans as I always make about horse shows and hunter trials, and I thought, there's still lots of the holidays left, if only Phantom gets well soon. Outside, the hills were all yellow with gorse and I cursed my foot because until it was better I wouldn't be able to ride. Presently, Dad turned round to call into the back, "By the way, I'm not being sent abroad again for five years, and you'll be grown-up by then."

I thought, I don't want to grow up. I want to stay the same for ever. I felt tremendously happy just to be alive ... to have Phantom, and to be going home.

Other titles in
THE PHANTOM HORSE series
£1.95

No. 1 Phantom Horse
No. 2 Phantom Horse Comes Home
No. 4 Phantom Horse In Danger
No. 5 Phantom Horse Goes To Scotland
No. 6 Wait For Me Phantom Horse

All these books are available at your local bookshop or news-agent, or can be ordered direct from the publisher. Just tick the titles you require and fill in the form below. Prices and availability subject to change without notice.

Ravette Books Limited, 3 Glenside Estate, Star Road, Partridge Green, Horsham, West Sussex RH13 8RA

Please send a cheque or postal order and allow the following for postage and packing. UK: 45p for up to two books and 15p for each additional book.

Name ....

Address ....

....